Aidan McQuade was CEO of Anti-Slavery International from 2006 to 2017, and prior to that worked extensively in development and humanitarian response for thirteen years. He comes from South Armagh in Ireland, and now lives in London.

THE
UNDISCOVERED
COUNTRY

Aidan McQuade

unbound

First published in 2020

Unbound

6th Floor Mutual House, 70 Conduit Street, London W1S 2GF

www.unbound.com

© Aidan McQuade, 2020

Extract from *North* by Seamus Heaney reproduced
by permission of Faber and Faber Ltd.

Text design and typesetting by Tetragon, London

A CIP record for this book is available from the British Library

ISBN 978-1-78352-807-3 (trade pbk)
ISBN 978-1-78352-808-0 (ebook)
ISBN 978-1-78352-815-8 (limited edition)

Printed and bound in Great Britain by Clays Ltd, Elcograf S.p.A.

1 3 5 7 9 8 6 4 2

For Klara,
who wanted to know what happened next,
with all my love

With special thanks to Eva Horelova

I am Hamlet the Dane,
skull-handler, parablist,
smeller of rot
in the state

—SEAMUS HEANEY,
Viking Dublin: Trial Pieces

Historical Note

THE IRISH WAR of Independence (1916–21) began with the Easter Rebellion, which was bloodily suppressed in Dublin after a week. Following this, the United Kingdom general election in 1918 returned a landslide victory in Ireland for Sinn Féin, who had contested the election on the promise of establishing an Irish parliament in Dublin, Dáil Éireann. The establishment of this parliament and a revolutionary government under the presidency of Eamon de Valera all but made certain that fighting would be renewed. The first shots were fired in 1919 with fighting reaching its peak in the second half of 1920 and the first half of 1921.

The Republican Courts were established in 1920 by Dáil Éireann, as a means of giving more concrete expression to the nascent Irish Republic. These operated across Ireland through the latter part of the War of Independence and the subsequent Truce period, notably in the west and south, areas from which British administration had, substantially, been driven.

Preface

TO: Colonel Daniel Long
Officer in Charge
Bureau of Military History
Dublin

7 Sept 1953

<u>HIGHLY CONFIDENTIAL</u>

Further to our conversation of Friday, 4 Sept 1953, please find attached, as I mentioned, the most problematic portion of former Volunteer Michael Gerard McAlinden, of Killean, County Armagh's submission to the Bureau.

Even with the moratorium on publication of these testimonies, until after all witnesses have passed away, I am of the opinion that this particular account should never see the light of day. Even if one could forgive the revolting coarseness of the language that former Volunteer McAlinden uses, something which I find hard to do, and the lurid, 'pulp-fiction' style of his narrative, his testimony casts shocking and unsubstantiated aspersions on the reputations of major figures in both our recent history and contemporary society.

I appreciate that the purpose of the Bureau is only to gather the testimonies of veterans of our War of Independence, and

I

that it leaves the task of assessing these accounts to future historians. But I, for one, feel that former Volunteer McAlinden is a voice that there is no need to hear, and the sort of filth that he has authored has no place in our national story.

Respectfully,

CAPTAIN JOSEPH WATERS
SENIOR ARCHIVIST

Ballykennedy,
Mayo, West of Ireland

NOVEMBER 1920

MONDAY

I

THE TREE WAS in the river and the kid was in the tree. The water, flooded with the freezing rains of winter, was black and fast-flowing. It shrivelled my balls just to look at it.

Eamon turned to me and asked, 'Do you swim?'

'Aye, a bit.'

'Right so! You'll go get him.' He turned to Packy O'Reilly and said, 'We need a decent rope, twenty yards or more. Do you have that yourself or know where you can get it?'

'I do,' said Packy.

'Well, hurry the fuck up then,' said Eamon, and Packy threw his arse over his saddle, and cycled off as fast as his blubbery gut would let him.

The kid couldn't have been more than ten or eleven. He looked like a ragdoll caught in the branches.

'First dead body?' asked Eamon.

'No,' I said, 'but first one that young.'

II

In spite of being a ginger, Dr Sophia Hennessy was a fine-looking woman. About thirty, she had green eyes, high cheekbones, and alabaster skin. The sort of woman who could tempt the pope, you'd imagine, what with all them pictures of redheads that Botticelli fella used to knock up for the Borgias and their pals.

The doctor was a Dublin Protestant, who had come to these parts when she had married her husband, sadly now dead, who had owned a substantial farm just outside town. She was, however, rumoured to sympathise with the Nationalist or Labour Party before the war, depending on who you were talking to, and there were tales of her agitating for votes for women. But none of this altered much her disdain for IRA men like ourselves, which she didn't bother to disguise, even those of us who had caught the shite duty of Republican Police.

She was doubly pissed off with us then, that we were intruding into her surgery and her routine of expectant mothers and poorly kids. Eamon introduced me as we sat down. She didn't bother to shake my hand when I offered it to her.

'What do you want?' She was a brusque one.

I sat down uncomfortably. My underpants were still wet through from my efforts to pull Liam from the entanglement of the hawthorn. I could feel myself soaking into the leather of the doctor's visitor chair. I hoped the water would ruin it.

'I don't want to take up too much of your time, Doctor, but we need your professional opinion,' said Eamon.

'Why's that then? Are you unsure whether or not you blew off some poor gobshite's knees and you want me to check?'

'Ah, very droll, Doctor,' said Eamon. 'But if only it were so simple.'

'What is it then?'

'We dragged the body of a child out of the river this morning. He was caught in a tree that had fallen into the river as a result of the recent rains. Frankly, it was pure luck that we found him. If he hadn't got caught in the branches he'd be halfway to the Atlantic Ocean by now.'

'Who was it?'

'It is not yet conclusive, Doctor, but preliminary identifications suggest the young fellow is Liam Finnegan, of Ballinamuck townland.'

She caught her breath.

'Sorry, Doctor. I presume you knew him?' I asked.

'I did,' she said. 'I've treated the whole family. Jesus, his poor mother.'

'We'll be needing you to have a final professional look at him then, Doctor,' said Eamon.

'Why?' she asked. 'If he's dead he's a case for Toner now.' Toner also ran an undertaking business adjacent to his pub.

'Like it or not, Doctor, we have our duties as Republican Police in these parts,' Eamon said.

She snorted her derision. 'Well, if you're going to be playing cops and robbers, I could think of a few dead people you should be worrying about, couldn't I?' She paused, as if awaiting an answer. When none came, she continued. 'But these days your lot are not too keen on folk taking any sort of interest in the causes of death around here, particularly a professional one.'

Eamon was quiet. I had found that he was not a man who was too often at a loss for words but for a moment he seemed to be choosing carefully what he wanted to say.

'Doctor, you may be aware that a few years ago I followed the advice of our parliamentary leadership and joined up to fight for the rights of small nations.'

'I've heard it said,' she said.

'Well, one afternoon, as I was taking in the sights of plucky little Belgium, I met a young German fella, who was doing much the same. Our relationship was brief but tragic, and, for reasons that I won't bore you with just now, I was compelled to leave the poor youngster dead in the mud.'

I could see the horror of the image flickering across Dr Hennessy's face, but she kept her composure. I imagine as a doctor she had heard her fair share of horror stories. 'Well, that's a grand story. I can rest assured now that I see the rich heritage of literary Ireland is safe in the hands of a new generation.'

'Doctor,' said Eamon, 'I have seen a lot of violent death in the civilising ranks of the British Army, but that is the only time I've seen a person who died from strangulation. That is, I think, until today.'

III

We came out of the surgery and leaned against the wall. Eamon lit a cigarette and breathed in.

'Jesus. She's a cranky one,' I said.

'Aye,' said Eamon. 'A redhead.'

'Have you had much dealings with her before?'

'She treated my mother when she was ill earlier this year. She was very good with her, no doubt about that. And me ma thinks the world of her. I've never found her the friendliest, but I suppose there's no rule says you have to like everybody.'

'Didn't Jesus say there was?'

'True enough, I suppose. But even Jesus had his limits.'

'Did he?'

'Well, I suspect those gombeen money-changers he kicked the shite out of didn't feel much of his love on them.'

Eamon took another puff on his cigarette.

'What made you think the young fella had been strangled?'

'That German lad that I killed. I spent what seemed like a very long time looking into his eyes when he died. That is not something that you easy forget, I can promise you. Liam's eyes looked the same to me. And then I found bruising on his throat.'

Eamon took a deep drag on his cigarette and then tossed the butt across the street. A cascade of sparks rose and died on the pavement.

'Well, no putting it off any longer,' he said.

'What?'

'Telling the family.'

We lifted our bicycles from against the wall and began the two miles to the Finnegan farm. It was unpleasant going, against the wind, but for once I was grateful at the delay this caused. I was not looking forward to seeing the family.

The Finnegan farmhouse was a poor-looking place with ageing thatch and the woodwork in desperate need of a lick of fresh paint.

A woman I presumed to be Liam's mother was in the kitchen baking when we arrived in the yard. She smiled when she came to the door and got as far as offering us a cup of tea before we – I mean Eamon, of course – summoned the resolve to tell her that we had just dragged her son from the river and that he was dead. Then it was as if her bones turned to water and she slumped to the bare stone floor of the kitchen.

A girl of fourteen or fifteen, with loose, shoulder-length brown hair and a dirty dress, I presumed a daughter, appeared in the kitchen and ran to her mother. I thought at first she was going to help her up, but instead she sank to the floor beside her. They grasped each other in a desperate hug and started to keen in unison. That set the baby wailing. It was an unholy cacophony of despair.

The father was out at the fields. There was no one about who seemed fit to get him so we had to wait.

After an hour or so he came strolling into the yard with a dog at his heels. He was smiling. The crying had died down out of exhaustion more than anything else so he had no inclination that anything was wrong until he saw the two of us leaning against his back wall.

That was the moment I saw the bottom fall out of the poor man's world.

IV

Dr Hennessy did the examination that evening in the back of Toner's undertakers. I would as soon have missed it, but Eamon insisted I watch, saying my interrupted legal training might come in useful.

I felt a bit queasy from the start. I had seen dead bodies before but only at wakes where death was softened by candle-light and they were lain out as if asleep in the front parlour amongst family and friends. This was an altogether harsher reality. Liam was stripped naked and stretched out on a table surrounded by an array of lamps. Dr Hennessy was laying out her shining steel surgical instruments. It sent a shiver down my spine.

Still, I felt I bore up okay at the start. At least, that is, until Dr Hennessy actually started cutting into the body. Then I threw up.

Eamon managed to hand me a bucket just as my mouth began to overflow. 'I thought this might come in useful,' he said.

Dr Hennessy looked up only briefly and said, 'For fuck sake.'

I would like to have been able to tell Eamon to go fuck himself but the contents of my guts were in my mouth.

After I finished, Eamon said, 'Okay, Mick. Go and wait in the pub and I'll see you when we are done. Try and get us a snug.' Dr Hennessy had barely hesitated with her work. The crack of the bones of Liam's ribcage speeded my departure.

An hour or so later, Eamon strode into the back of the pub, shouted for a pint over the ruckus of the throng in the public bar, and then slumped heavily onto the bench in the snug beside me.

'I told you I didn't fucking want to go into that examination,' I said.

'Fuck sake, Mick. I don't know if it passed your attention, but we are in the midst of a war at the moment. If you are going to be upset at that sort of thing I do genuinely worry for your life expectancy.'

We were both quiet for a moment.

'You didn't offer to buy the doctor a drink, what with her service to the Republic just now?'

'Jaysus. Things must be different in the Black North. Folks round here don't like to see women in pubs.'

'I thought that was why God created snugs.'

'Ah no, Mick. They were created so that men could hide away more safely.'

'Well, the language on Dr Hennessy suggests she is a more broad-minded sort, who has perhaps encountered more than one pub in the course of that university education of hers, and, hmm, I don't know, just having hacked open the body of a child, I thought she might need a drink.'

'Aye. So did I. But, to be honest, I think she would prefer to drink with shite-covered pigs than socialise with the likes of us.'

'So where is she now?'

'She is helping Toner make the body a bit more respectable for the family. They are waiting out front to take the body home for the wake.'

'I should have asked you earlier, but did you know the young fella?'

'Not so much. I know the family. His da was well ahead of me at school. No interest in politics but good neighbours. The sort of folk who would help you out if you were stuck. No fuss like. The young fella, Liam, he did a bit in Bruton's in his summer holidays and at weekends, stacking shelves and the like. So I'd have seen him about from time to time.'

'So what did youse find out?' I asked.

'Well,' said Eamon, 'a lot of stuff that's not good. As well as the extensive bruising that I saw around his throat, there was no water in the young fella's lungs.'

'So she thinks the kid was strangled too?'

Eamon grunted.

'Have you told the family your suspicions?'

'No. And the doctor is under strict instructions to keep her gob shut as well. No point in distressing the poor family further to no avail.'

He took a slug from his pint.

'Where's the chess set?' Eamon asked.

'In my bag,' I said.

'Well, get it out, for fuck sake!'

I did and we set up the board. 'My turn on white,' I said. Eamon led me twenty-three games to three in the series. I won exclusively when Eamon was somewhat the worse for wear, and he had compensated for those almost immediately by demanding a rematch, which he won. So, while I really wasn't in his league, chess players were few enough on the ground in these parts. Eamon knew it would be churlish to complain about my quality: it was a choice between me or nothing.

We set up the pieces and began moving, both our open-ings well practised. Eamon played with an unsettlingly rapid tempo as we moved into the middle game. 'Chess is like life,' he would say from time to time, 'if you have to kill something it's best not to fuck about.'

'So who would do such a thing?' I asked after moving a knight.

'Some sick bastard. Dr Hennessy also found ligature marks around his wrists and substantial bruising around his mouth, suggesting he was bound and gagged.'

'Why would somebody tie him up like that?'

'Well, I'm not an expert,' said Eamon, moving a pawn on the flank, 'but I suspect it may mess up your *joie de vivre* some-what to have a kid screaming and struggling uncomfortably as you try to fuck him.'

'What?'

'There was evidence that he had been sexually assaulted.'

'What?' I repeated.

'Sorry, Mick. I don't mean to be coy, but I thought you were an educated man. Don't they tell you about such things in your criminal law and evidence classes in that university of yours in Galway?'

I took a mouthful of my pint. 'They tend to use euphemisms for such things.'

'That's the way the doctor described it. I don't get the sense she has much time for euphemisms.'

'Well,' I said moving my queen's bishop to the middle of the board, 'in answer to your question I've heard tell of such things in Dublin and London. But this is bleeding Mayo.'

'Indeed it is. So who would do such a thing? And to make matters worse there are few enough of either British or West British types in these parts who might be given to such perversions.'

'Might he not have been picked up by some sadist from the Crown forces?'

'I would think if there had been Black and Tans about this morning we'd all have known about it, don't you?'

'What about Father Crosby? I heard he's a Dub.'

'Aye, he's from the Pale, all right. Fucking Jackeen,' said Eamon moving a knight to take one of my pawns.

'And Dr Hennessy.'

'Aye, her too… I reckon she's probably very dirty, but in a good way.'

'Oh dear Lord. Do we know anything else from the medical examination?'

'Time of death was difficult to determine because of his time in the water. But Dr Hennessy did find that his stomach contents included potatoes, carrots and some form of meat. That would have been his last meal. He died sometime between that and us hauling him out of the water. And somebody who he met in that time period killed him.'

'I think I read somewhere that these sorts of crimes are usually committed by someone who knows the victim.' There was a knight going begging in my half of the board so I took it with a pawn. It was a rare error on Eamon's part, I thought. He must have been distracted.

'Where did you read that?'

'Wasn't it Freud?'

'What did he say?'

'He wrote about the experiences of rape and incest amongst his patients in Vienna, I think.'

'I thought that dirty bastard recanted everything.'

'He might have done for all I know. I'm no expert. I only read a couple of articles about it. I found it all quite distressing.'

'It might have been helpful if you'd had the stomach for more.'

'No fixing that now, unfortunately.'

'Aye.'

We sat for a while, contemplating the enormity of what Dr Hennessy had found.

'There is something rotten here,' said Eamon.

'Jesus,' I said. 'Where the fuck are the police when you need them?'

Eamon said nothing. Then placed his fingers on his queen, picked it up and set it down beside my king. 'Checkmate,' he said.

That startled me.

'Fucker,' I said, and checked the board to see if he was right. He was. The hanging knight had been part of an elaborate trap that I had fallen into and it infuriated me that I'd been foxed again. But the formalities had to be observed. I extended my hand to Eamon. He shook it. 'You know, Mick,' he said, 'that very thought did pass my mind as I was watching the lovely Dr Hennessy carving up young Liam.'

'The "Where are the police when you need them?" thought?'

'Aye,' said Eamon, 'that one. Of course, due to the circumstances in which we find ourselves, that is fucking us.'

V

We finished our pints and then at Eamon's suggestion went back to Peter McLaughlin's solicitor's office, where we had a sort of a professional base. Despite it being almost eight o'clock, McLaughlin was still there. Bronagh, his freckled, brown-eyed secretary, had already long gone home.

He was looking a bit harassed, but I always found him to be courtesy itself. He carried a certain melancholy about him, so I wasn't surprised when Eamon told me once his only son had been killed in France in 1915. 'Well,' said Eamon, 'he was actually declared "missing in action", which caused some unfortunate hope. It was my luck to draw the shitty straw when I was home on leave of having to tell his da that "missing in action" meant he had suffered a direct hit by a German shell and was reduced to bloody dust which no one could ever identify. I put it a bit more gently than that, of course. I told his da it was instantaneous and he wouldn't have known a thing. That may have been some comfort to him and the wife.'

Comfort or not, McLaughlin's wife had died shortly after and, with no other children, there was little left for McLaughlin apart from the work. And the horses. He had a particular passion for horse racing. Horses notwithstanding, he must have been pleased enough to be asked to chair the parish court in the new Dáil court system. It was more work for him.

Along with Dáil Éireann itself, the courts were one of the concrete manifestations of the Republic that we were now all supposed to be trying to create. Since the increased support for the national movement over the past two years, and particularly with the IRA offensive of the summer and autumn just passed which had pushed the police and British administration from large parts of the west, and into fortified positions in the bigger towns like Castlebar, the opportunity for extending the civil reach of the Dáil had increased. So it had been decided in Dublin to create a new court system to replace, where possible, the Crown's judicial apparatus. And, in this part of Mayo at least, much of the business that had previously been handled by the British court system had now been taken over by the Dáil courts.

The work of the parish court was routine enough stuff. It had jurisdiction for claims not in excess of £10 in contract and tort, and summary criminal jurisdiction in relation to some petty offences. But it was more than that for McLaughlin. It was work in the service of the Irish Republic. Work against the British Empire, which he blamed for killing his son by selling us all a false bill of goods over Home Rule in order to boost the recruitment of Irish Volunteers into the British Army. I suspect if he was not so old and portly McLaughlin may have been tempted now to take up arms with the IRA himself in order to hasten the British Empire's demise.

I heard down Toner's that years before McLaughlin had done some criminal defence work, including a murder trial, the details of which seemed to shift and shimmer with each telling, or perhaps with each pint. But for now most of his legal work dealt with conveyancing, property and contractual disputes.

I thought there was probably considerable scope for conflict of interest with his role on the parish court, but Peter seemed like a scrupulous and principled man. 'Just because there is a war on doesn't mean we can just say, "To hell with it and devil take the hindmost",' he said to me when he was briefing me on my role in the court's service. 'We must show that the rule of law remains paramount if we want to "take our place amongst the nations of the earth", as Parnell put it.'

I knew from reading McLaughlin's copy of the constitution of the court that there was provision for a member of the clergy to be appointed to the court. But, Eamon had told me, when McLaughlin had approached Father Crosby he told McLaughlin to get lost, and not even politely, which was the thing that surprised me most given McLaughlin's studious good manners.

There were few enough takers for roles in the Republican court system, which was understandable. If you were going to risk hard labour or worse if the British got their hands on you, you would probably want to be doing something more exciting than the boring and mundane fare the parish court offered. So Peter's potential conflicts of interest or not, I presumed the largely imaginary republic that we sought to serve couldn't really be too choosy.

'Could we have a word please, Peter,' said Eamon.

'Course you can. Sit down, boys. A sad day it's been, I hear. Young Finnegan?'

'Aye, Liam Finnegan.'

'Jesus. His poor family. What happened? Mitching off school and got into trouble?'

'I don't think so, Peter. Dr Hennessy has concluded an examination and confirmed my initial suspicion that foul play was involved.'

'Explain yourself there please, Eamon.'

'There were certain things about the body I found unsettling. So we asked Dr Hennessy to have a closer look.'

'And?'

'And she confirmed my original suspicions: that Liam was strangled. It is unclear to us at present how he got in the water, but he did not die of drowning. My belief is that whoever killed him put him in the river in order to conceal his crime. If Liam hadn't been caught in the tree that we pulled him out of, God alone knows when he would have been found.'

'Jesus,' said McLaughlin. Then he said it again. 'Jesus.'

I waited for Eamon to mention the sexual assault, but he said nothing.

McLaughlin leaned back in his chair and reached in his desk to take out a battered packet of cigarettes and a box of matches. He lit one and then threw the packet to me. I didn't smoke so I passed the packet to Eamon who took one and then set the cigarette packet back on McLaughlin's desk.

'What sort of a fucker would hurt a child like that?' he asked.

'We have been asking ourselves the same question. The only thing we have managed to come up with, courtesy of Mick's recent studies, is that it was likely done by someone already known to the victim.'

'Jesus,' said McLaughin and took a drag on his cigarette. 'It wasn't maybe some Tans lifted him for some sort of sadistic amusement?' he asked.

'I think we'd have heard about it if they'd been out and about this morning. Looks like they're sitting tight in Castlebar, and hopefully we won't see those fuckers again before spring.'

McLaughlin took another long pull on his cigarette while we said nothing.

'Listen,' McLaughlin said, suddenly animated. 'The court system established by the Ministry of Home Affairs of the Dáil Éireann has not empowered the parish courts to have jurisdiction on any but the most petty of criminal offences. However, we are empowered to investigate, take evidence and return the accused for trial before the district court at the circuit sitting. The first circuit sitting is in three weeks' time, in Ballina. What do you think you boys can find out between now and then?'

'Probably not a lot,' said Eamon. 'We're hardly Scotland Yard. I mean, if there was a league table for shite detectives in Western Europe we would probably be at the top of it.'

'Aye,' said Peter, 'but while ye may be incompetent, ye are not stupid. And that's the best I have at the moment.'

'It could be argued that this exceeds the authority granted to a parish court by Dáil Éireann,' I said. 'Do you think your fellow court members will be okay with us poking into this matter?'

'A word of advice, Mick,' said McLaughlin. ''Tis better to ask forgiveness than to seek permission.'

TUESDAY

VI

IT WOULD BE stretching a point to say we left McLaughlin's that night with a plan. We left with an agreement to go to Liam's wake the next day and see if could get any notion of when he had those spuds, carrots and unidentified meat, and if anybody had any idea of what he had been doing between then and us fishing him out of the water.

We were both somewhat the worse for wear the next day, so we finally headed to the Finnegan farm in the late morning. Neighbours and extended family had arrived out in force and were making tea and sandwiches.

We were shown into the best room at the front of the house – such rooms got little use except for wakes. The room was clean, but poorly furnished. In fact, it seemed to me that the coffin was the most expensive item in the place. Paddy Toner had delivered the body back to the family the night before and Liam would lie with them until taken to the church for his burial the next day.

The doctor and Toner had done a good job with him after the depredations of the post-mortem exam. Liam was stretched out as if asleep, a black rosary threaded through his fingers and his face lit by candles set around his five-foot coffin.

'Eternal rest grant unto him O Lord, and let perpetual light shine upon him,' I prayed to myself as I looked upon the face of the dead child. He was a nice-looking kid, still with some puppy fat on his face. I felt the involuntary prickle of tears in my eyes.

I turned from the coffin and saw that Eamon was already strolling out into the hallway, saying hello to someone, a neighbour or old school friend.

I wanted a cup of tea, but decided that I really should first pay my respects to the family. They were sitting together in another downstairs room in their Sunday best, greeting neighbours who had come to express their sympathies. I queued up to wait my turn.

'Very sorry for your trouble, Mrs Finnegan, Mr Finnegan,' I said when my turn came. It always struck me as a singularly unimaginative thing to say, but I never managed to come up with anything better. My da once said, 'Not to worry, son. In times like these your presence is more important than your words.'

'That's good of you, son,' Liam's father said almost without thinking, just playing out his part of the routine. But something caused him pause. 'I'm sorry, but how do I know you?' he asked. I noticed that the cuffs of his suit were frayed.

'We met yesterday when myself and my comrade brought the news.'

He blinked and then seemed to remember. 'I'm sorry,' he said. 'It was something of a shock for me. Most of yesterday is a bit of a blur to me now.'

'No need to apologise at all,' I said. 'I can only imagine how dreadful it must have been. I'm so sorry to have been the bearer of such bad news.'

'You are not from these parts,' he asked.

'I'm not. I am from South Armagh. But I'm serving here with the Republican Police. I wish we could have met under happier circumstances.'

'We all do, son,' he said and Mrs Finnegan stifled a sob.

'When was the last time you saw Liam?' I asked.

'Yesterday morning. He was up with me at sunrise to bring the cows in for milking and then he left to serve at early Mass.'

'That would have been, what, about half past seven?'

'Aye, about then.'

'Would he normally come home before going to school?'

'No. Brigid' – he tilted his head in the direction of his wife – 'made him a ham sandwich to have after Mass. She would always make sure he had something with him to eat when he was serving.'

'So you wouldn't have expected him home until after school?'

'Aye. About the time you and your pal showed up yesterday.'

'Very sorry for your troubles,' I said again, and shook hands with the mother and father, and then gave a slight bow towards the brown-haired daughter – Maire was her name, Eamon had told me – who was cradling the baby in her arms.

It was only now I wondered what the name of the baby was but I thought it was too late to ask.

I wandered into the kitchen and a young black-haired woman gave me a cup of tea and a very pretty girl of about ten offered me a ham sandwich. I was feeling a bit claustrophobic, knowing no one in the crowded kitchen, so I took the tea and bap into the backyard.

It was raining but small knots of men were gathered there sheltering under eaves or beside gable walls, chatting and smoking. I strained to see anybody I recognised. There were a few Volunteers, but my familiarity with them was limited since, when I arrived in these parts barely over a month ago, I had been detached from the battalion and told to report to Peter McLaughlin. That is where I met Eamon who described our duty as 'providing a bit of muscle to McLaughlin in case some gobshite thinks he can ignore the esteemed judgement of the Court.'

I recognised one of the Volunteers, Shamey O'Neill, standing to one side of the farmyard, having a smoke. He was one of the few Volunteers whose name I knew.

'How's it going, Shamey?' I asked.

'You still in Ballykennedy, McAlinden? I would have thought by now you would have gone back up north to your unionist friends there.'

I was taken aback a bit, but I shouldn't have been. I had spoken with Shamey once before, but I had forgotten just how stupid and offensive a clown he actually was. Shamey was one of those people so comfortable in their own ignorance that even the hardest and most pristine of facts could never penetrate the ocean of stupid with which he surrounded his view of the world. I suspected he believed with a considerable vehemence that everyone from the north was a Protestant, and that all Protestants were Unionists. I suspected this belief was so profound that as far as he was concerned both Charles Stewart Parnell and Wolfe Tone, if he had ever heard of them, had not only been sincere Catholics but probably daily communicants too. It would not have surprised me if I had discovered he also believed that the earth was flat and borne through the cosmos on the back of an enormous turtle, given that Isaac Newton was both English and Protestant and sure you could never be trusting the likes of them.

'I am grateful to whoever invented the word "gobshite", Shamey. It makes it a lot easier when speaking about you.'

Some folk in Mayo, I know, claimed to have difficulty with my northern accent. But in Shamey's case I am not sure he had ever properly grasped the concept of language. I left him with his mouth hanging open, probably trying to remember how to chew, when I walked off.

I managed a couple of steps towards a small group of other Volunteers sheltering against the wall of a pigsty when I heard a different voice from over my shoulder.

'Volunteer McAlinden!' It made me start and I spun round to face him. Commandant Jack O'Riordain, Officer Commanding the 5th Mayo (Ballykennedy) battalion of the Irish Republican Army. The man who had assigned me to the Republican Police. O'Riordain was a big and powerfully built man. He was a good three or four inches taller than me, and I was almost six feet tall.

'Commandant!' I said, snapping to something resembling attention. It went through my mind if I should salute. I decided against it, given the circumstances, not least that my hands were full of tea and baps.

'What brings you here?' he asked.

'Paying my respects to the family.'

'You made their acquaintance in the brief time you have been amongst us?'

'Only yesterday, Commandant. 'Twas us who recovered the body.'

'Recovered from where?'

'The river, about a mile outside of town. He'd got caught in the branches of a fallen tree.'

'Fell in messing about, I suppose.'

'It would certainly look that way.'

We stood in silence for a moment. Then I asked, 'You must have known him, Commandant?'

'I did,' O'Riordain said. 'I've known him for the better part of six years since he first came to my school.'

In addition to commanding the local battalion, O'Riordain was headmaster at the local primary school.

'What was he like?'

'A very bright child but awkward. Advanced reading age. Dreadful handwriting. Decent arithmetic. Completely useless at football.'

'He didn't show up at school yesterday?'

'No. I only realised that when I took the roll call. But I thought nothing of it. I just thought he must have been home with the snifters or maybe mitching off.'

27

'Was he the sort of young fellow to normally mitch off school and go rambling in the countryside?'

'He wasn't, but he'd developed an enthusiasm for Robert Louis Stevenson recently, you know those Highland stories, *Kidnapped* and the rest. Sort of thing that might stir the imagination to look for a new little adventure.'

'What did you do when you realised he was missing?'

'I asked the class if anyone knew where he was.'

'Did they?'

'No. But that's not so unusual, you know yourself. Youngsters are always picking up all sorts of bugs. If he'd missed two days in a row I would have visited his parents.'

I wondered if there was something else I should ask him, but drew a blank.

'So how are you settling in, Mick?' O'Riordain asked.

'Not so bad. Mr McLaughlin keeps us busy, and the Bonners, who I'm staying with, are very good to me.'

'Glad to hear it, Mick. It's difficult times in which we live. It's good to hear that you are making the best that can be expected in the circumstances. It's a bit different from the student life, isn't it?'

''Tis. But I'm used to this sort of thing. I grew up on a farm outside Newry.'

'It's a long way from the Black North to the West of Ireland.'

''Tis, but poor Catholics have it the same all over Ireland.' That was becoming a familiar refrain from me, how things aren't that different on the east coast compared to the west, that there was, really, only one Ireland even if there were a multitude of accents and a diversity of religions.

'Dundalk is as far north as I ever made it. I had an interview for a school there just after I graduated.'

'Didn't get it?'

'Didn't fancy it. Still too much of the small town about it, though it's bigger than Ballykennedy. I wanted to work in the city for a while.'

'Do you miss it? Dublin?'

'Not so much. You get your fill of that sort of thing after a bit. I had a yearning for home.'

'I don't imagine Shamey O'Neill has ever had a yearning for anything but home.'

'Why do you say that?'

'He has a certain suspicion of anything he is unfamiliar with, and he has some strange notions.'

'You mean regarding yourself?'

'He seems to regard me as some creature with the evil eye.'

'We are a small town, right enough, and not as cosmopolitan as Dublin, or even Galway for that matter. But we pride ourselves on our hospitality. Still, that might have taken a bit of a dint now that we are also in a time of war. Shamey's exercised by the thought that spies and informers might wreck this independence struggle as they have every other for the past three hundred years.'

'I'm no fucking informer!'

'Aye. So you say. But I imagine if you were an informer that's exactly what you would say too. And maybe I've read too many penny dreadfuls in my youth but aren't you always meant to be a bit suspicious of the one that gets away?'

'What does that mean?'

'Police raid on your digs but you happen to avoid it, out of pure luck, you say, and that gives you an excuse to fetch up in our midst here? I was a student myself once, so I won't deny your story rings true to me. But to Shamey, and some others like him who don't have the experience of being students, it seems a bit of a convenient story.'

'Nor the experience of reading, I would have thought, even penny dreadfuls.'

'Ach, Shamey's not the worst. He's the heart of a lion and loyal to a fault.'

'But where does that leave me? Do I just have to come to terms with living under their suspicion for the rest of my days, or at least for the rest of my days here?'

'Just keep doing what you are doing: your job. And keep doing it well. Eventually people will come around. We may seem a little stand-offish at the moment, but the people of this parish are as decent as any in Ireland.'

'Hmm,' I said.

'Here's your partner in crime so,' said O'Riordain, as Eamon strolled up to join us. Eamon was always a man careful about his priorities. He had also snagged a cup of tea and a ham sandwich.

'Commandant,' said Eamon. It was plain from Eamon's demeanour that the thought of saluting had simply not crossed his mind.

'Gleason,' the Commandant responded. 'Well, I don't want to be keeping you two fellows from your pressing duties, and I must pay my respects to the family. So I will wish you both good day.' And with that he turned on his heel and entered the house.

'Cunt,' Eamon snorted, and took a chunk out of his bap.

VII

'So what have you got against O'Riordain?'

We were back in the kitchen of McLaughlin's office. Eamon was sitting on a straight back chair, his feet, still in their hobnailed boots, resting up on the kitchen table, and another mug of tea clenched in his fist as he reclined back in his chair. He was in his late twenties, fit-looking and always clean-shaven, with sandy-coloured hair flecked with grey about the temples, and startlingly pale-blue eyes. I'm not sure I would have described him as handsome, but he had an intelligent face. The first time I met him I thought 'a lean and hungry look' but that disappeared when he smiled, or when he had a few pints – they often went hand in hand.

'He's a cunt,' said Eamon.

'I am aware of that. But why do you think so?'

'I was at school with him. He was a cunt then too.'

'So how did such a cunt end up as commandant of the local battalion of the IRA?'

'Well, he does have a certain credibility, having been one of the few Volunteers in these parts who wasn't gobshite enough to follow Redmond's urgings to France.'

'Unlike you.'

'Unlike me.'

'He has always been very civil to me,' I said.

'He may have been,' said Eamon, 'but he told Peter to let him know if you so much as farted funny.'

'Why was he so interested in the timbre of my farts?'

'The usual reason, I suppose. Because you're a northerner.'

'What's that got to do with anything?'

'I suppose if you look at it from his point of view, Mick. You are a man from God knows where, and it is his job to be suspicious. Look at how many revolutionary movements in our past have been destroyed by informers.'

'I've heard that oul shite already from O'Riordain this morning. Is that all you folk talk about around here, whether I'm an informer and whether youse should have me shot?'

'I'm just telling you what O'Riordain said. I don't think you can accuse either Peter or me of sizing you up for a coffin just yet.'

'So why didn't you say something about it earlier?'

'Honestly, Mick, I didn't think about it.'

'So why do you tell me now?'

'I suppose it's because it's modest evidence that he's a bit of a two-faced cunt.'

I didn't say anything. From one perspective I could see O'Riordain's suspicion was reasonable. But it still made me upset. For one thing it meant the source of Shamey's, and indeed everyone else's suspicions about me appeared to be our very own commander.

'I suppose Jack can't help himself. He must be jealous of that superior intelligence and proficiency as lovers that us northerners are famed for.'

'Gobshite,' Eamon said.

'I really don't think you can be calling me a gobshite when fucking eejits like Shamey O'Neill walk amongst us.'

'That,' said Eamon, 'is an extremely good point, Mick. It's true Shamey is a particularly special case. He is the one single piece of evidence we have that Jack O'Riordain not only has a sense of humour, but is a comic genius of historic proportions. If Oscar Wilde was still alive he would be sitting at the feet of Jack O'Riordain taking notes. Fuck it: if Oscar Wilde were alive today he would have already killed himself because he would feel so utterly inadequate in the presence of such extraordinary greatness.'

'What do you mean?' I asked.

'Jack appointed Shamey intelligence officer to the battalion.'

'When?'

'A couple of weeks ago. Shortly after you came to join me and Peter in the elite ranks of the Republican Police.'

'Fuck!' I said. 'But the man is a complete fucking eejit.'

'Aye,' said Eamon, 'the words "Shamey" and "intelligence" are rarely to be found together in the same sentence. Can you imagine it: making someone of such a self-regarding level of stupidity intelligence officer? He probably holds it as a point of pride that he cannot even spell the title of the post he currently holds.'

'Why did Jack give him the job?'

'Jack likes always to be the one calling the shots. And if Shamey has one virtue it's that he'll keep his nose wedged firmly up Jack's arse.'

'I've met folk like him in Galway.'

'What? There are six-fingered, inbred gobshites wandering the streets of Galway?'

'Not so many of the six-fingered variety. But there certainly are enormous piles of gobshites who hate, as a point of principle, that which they have never known.'

'Ach, show a bit of understanding here, Mick. Ignorance has always been the soundest basis for prejudice.'

'Aye, that I understand. But it's them who regard their ignorant prejudice as wisdom that really get me.'

'They truly are God's special gift. The shining exemplars of stupid who provide all the evidence that you will ever need as to the importance of education.'

'You're a well-educated man, then,' I said.

'Senior certificate at the Christian Brothers, thank you very much!'

'No, it's more than that,' I said. 'You've been remarkably free from the snide comments regarding my origins since we met.'

'Two things I've learned in the school of life, Mick.'

'What are those, then?'

'First of all, where you hail from is little guide as to the quality of your character.'

'And second?'

'You have to watch out for your comrades.'

I said nothing and drank some tea.

'So what have we learned?' Eamon asked.

'Apart from Shamey being the biggest gobshite in Connaught, and Jack O'Riordain being Ireland's greatest comedic genius since Oscar Wilde?'

'Indeed apart from that. About Liam's death, I meant.'

34

'Well, the kid was out early to serve at Mass. His mother made him a ham sandwich for after. Didn't show up at school according to O'Riordain, who seems to have been the first person who realised he was missing when he took the roll. Says he didn't think much of it though – kids miss the odd day of school from time to time.'

'Doesn't appear to have eaten the sandwich either.'

'How the fuck do you know that?'

'His stomach, according to Dr Hennessy, did not have any bread.'

'Ah!'

'You know there is them say that university educations are a waste of money.'

'Fuck you.'

'That may be the best you can do, Mick, if your self-proclaimed capabilities as a lover are as underwhelming as your intellectual skills.'

Eamon drained his tea, swung his feet off the table and jumped up.

'Time to chat to Father Crosby so.'

VIII

Having checked at the parochial house we found Crosby shuffling around his vestry at the back of the church. He didn't disguise his impatience.

Father Martin Crosby was a good-looking man. In his late thirties, I would have guessed, with olive skin, jet-black hair and dark eyes. Dub or not, I thought he must have an infusion of some Spanish Armada blood somewhere in his family tree. Eamon said he was also a demon midfielder for the parish football team, which he still played in. I wondered was that how he got the bruising on his cheekbone.

'I have to get out to the Finnegan's, so if you can be quick about it!'

'Well, Father,' Eamon started. 'It's actually about that.'

'What?'

'The last time Liam Finnegan was seen alive was by his mother on his way out to serve your eight o'clock Mass.'

'It wasn't the last time he was seen alive. He arrived here at ten to eight and served the Mass. He left for school after tidying up here at about eight-thirty.'

'Anybody else confirm that?'

'I had a congregation of about ten. They had left by the time Liam did.'

Eamon said nothing, and looked at Crosby as if he was expecting him to say more. Eventually, the priest broke the silence. 'Mind if we step outside for a breath of air?' he asked.

We stepped out of the vestry door and Crosby lit a cigarette. He didn't offer any around. There was a patina of sweat on his forehead, and I noticed some recent scratches on the hand that held his cigarette. 'What's with all this Holmes and Watson shite?'

'What do you mean, Father?' I asked.

'A young fella dies in an apparent tragic accident and you boys are acting the Keystone Cops.'

'We are just trying to ascertain his final movements,' I said.

'See if we can find out where he went into the water in case there are some hazards there we can have removed. Stop further such tragic accidents in the future.'

'Ascertain?' said Crosby.

'Mick was a law student,' said Eamon. 'I heard him say "jurisprudence" once as well. But we've put a stop to that sorta shite now, haven't we, Mick.'

I said nothing and Crosby did not smile.

'He left here about eight-thirty. I offered him a cup of tea before he had to go to school. He said he'd need to be getting on. That is the last time I saw him until I saw his body in Toner's yesterday evening.'

'Well, we don't want to keep you any longer, Father. Many thanks.' Eamon offered his hand, but the priest turned and walked back into the vestry without another word.

As we walked away from the church towards the bridge over the river, Eamon asked me, 'Did you ever serve Mass as a youngster?'

'Of course,' I said.

'Priest ever offer you a cup of tea after?'

'Never,' I said.

'Aye. Me neither.'

IX

The bridge was a double-arched stone affair. If truth be told it was probably the most interesting thing about Ballykennedy. It was a place of about a thousand people, though many more lived in the rural hinterland. The main part of the village stretched up from the bridge to the church on the crest of the hill.

I wrote to my parents after I got here, while not naming it. There was only one thing to do here, I said, 'walk up the main street and then walk back down it. And once you have done that you have seen the place twice.'

'Still,' I added, 'there is a mountain outside of town and the locals say you can predict the weather from it: if you can see it, it means it's going to rain, and if you can't, it means it's raining.' My da told me the same thing about Slieve Gullion in South Armagh. I imagine the same joke was made in many parts of the world. But the telling of it again, in my semi-exile, stirred up a pang of home-sickness. It was my da's second favourite joke, right after the one about the man who didn't want to eat cow's tongue for his dinner because it came out of an animal's mouth, so he had a boiled egg instead.

We could see the mountain now, so it wasn't raining, and we leaned on the parapet and looked at the black water still in torrent. Eamon lit a cigarette, took a deep drag on it and then exhaled the cloud of smoke with a deep sigh.

'So what next?' I asked.

'Fuck sake. Why are you asking me? You're the bleeding law student. Didn't they mention anything in your fucking lectures?'

'Well, you're the veteran of foreign wars, a man of the world and distinguished graduate of the school of hard fucking knocks. I thought someone might have mentioned something to you while you were killing them?'

Eamon laughed at that. 'I haven't killed that many.'

'Enough to lose count, though.'

'That tends to happen if you fire a machine gun.'

We took another drag on our cigarettes.

'So no bright ideas?' asked Eamon.

'We could try to speak to his classmates, see if any of them saw or heard anything.'

'Aye. Most of them should be at the funeral tomorrow. We could have a chat with some of them then. Discreetly, mind. I still don't want us to broadcast our suspicions too widely.'

'So what between now and then?'

'Well, one thing we know is that he didn't go into the water by himself. So I think a stroll along the riverbank might not be the worst thing we could do.'

We took opposite banks and walked with the current down towards the tree where we found the kid. It was about a mile outside of town, which made it about a mile and a half below the bridge, on my side of the river. I found nothing out of the ordinary apart from the marks of our activity where we had pulled Liam out of the water. We then started back and walked up towards the bridge about a mile and a half upstream.

We soon lost sight of each other amid the stands of trees on the banks of the river.

If there was anything of any interest I thought that the grazing cattle would probably have trampled over it. But I agreed with Eamon that I couldn't think of anything better to be doing.

About half a mile up from the bridge I found some tyre tracks where a pasture swept low to a curve in the river. Beyond that nothing.

I tramped back down to the bridge and waited for Eamon. I got through a couple of boiled sweets before he returned.

'What kept you?' I asked.

'I walked a bit further.'

'Find anything?' I asked.

'Tyre tracks in two places.'

'I found some tyre tracks too. About half a mile upriver.'

'I found one other thing.' He lifted off his shoulder the satchel he habitually carried with him and opened the flap. He reached inside and drew out a sodden package of brown paper. It was tied loosely with string but enough paper had been torn away to see what was inside: the half-rotten remains of a sandwich, the ham still glistening pink.

X

'So who owns a car?'

We were standing next to the river, on a patch of soft meadow obscured from the road by trees where Eamon said he had found the remains of the sandwich. The tracks of a four-wheeled vehicle were still discernible in the grass and mud of the field.

'Well, whatever we may think of Commandant O'Riordain, he is an efficient sort. We took an inventory a few months back in case we had to commandeer one for the good of the Republic.'

'So do you know who was on the list?'

'I remember the list. It wasn't long and it was me who compiled it.'

'Well?'

'Six people: Sophia Hennessy, our delectable medical doctor; Jack O'Riordain himself; Dick Bruton, of the general store fame – actually, he has a small van rather than a car; Francie Quinn, our local livestock dealer, has both a car and a cattle truck, but that doesn't look to me like truck tracks; Peter McLaughlin, our boss, and Father Martin Crosby, our esteemed parish priest.'

'You don't think Peter could have done it, do you?' I asked.

'Well, I got to the office yesterday morning about ten o'clock and both you and he were already there. What time did you get there?'

'About half-nine. And he was there, as was Bronagh.'

'Bronagh tells me he normally comes in before her and she starts at nine. Sure we can ask her and see if we can eliminate him quick. So what strikes you about the rest?'

'You don't think a woman could have done this?'

'Call me prejudiced but it doesn't seem likely to me, what with her lacking the necessary accoutrements to sexually assault young Liam. Still in the name of thoroughness I suppose we should ask her a few questions.'

'What of the rest of them? Any of them seem like child murderers to you?'

'Of late you have passed comment on the absence of police in this vicinity.'

'They were rhetorical remarks, really. I mean you can still just about smell the petrol fumes from the shell of the old barracks.'

Eamon took a drag on his cigarette and turned to look into the black waters of the river.

'There were five RIC men in that barracks when we attacked it at the end of August, the sergeant and four constables. They put up a hell of a fight, but in the end we managed to set fire to the roof and they had no choice but to surrender. Two of them had been killed in the fight and one more of them had been shot up a bit but he'd have been okay with medical attention.'

Eamon paused and took another drag on his cigarette. I did not get the sense he was liking this story.

'O'Riordain ordered all the survivors to be executed. The whole lot of them are buried out the back of the barracks.'

I felt sick. 'You killed them after they surrendered?'

'O'Riordain and the others killed them. To be fair, their blood was up after the fight. The cops had killed three of ours in the course of the shooting and wounded a couple more. And the local RIC Sergeant, Finucane was his name, he was a complete cunt of long standing.'

'He's a dead cunt now.'

'He is.'

'You didn't join in?'

'No. I'd seen enough of that sort of thing in France. "Intolerant" treatment of the prisoners, the officers would call it, giving a nod and a wink to troops butchering prisoners as a way of "letting off steam". I've had to live with some of that, young Germans begging for their lives, chance to see their children or sweethearts again. Some of them probably to have their first shag. So I told O'Riordain he could fuck himself. Fat lot of good that did anyone. He transferred me to Peter and the Republican Police after that. Said I was bad for battalion morale.'

'You think he could abuse and kill a child?'

'Maybe. Maybe not. I didn't like the enthusiasm he took with those executions. But I've some of that sort of blood on my own hands. War does that to even the most decent of people. Anyway, I can't see him having the time or opportunity for that – rape and kill a kid between eight-thirty and nine and then teach a class full of other children their ABCs?'

'What of the others?'

'Bruton is harmless enough but has a streak of the gombeen in him. But I have never heard his name connected with violence of any sort. Quite the opposite: I heard he near shit himself the last time a drunk tried to pick a fight with him after a dance, and his dancing days are long past. Quinn has been known to butcher a few cattle. So he knows a bit about killing.'

'Which leaves us with Father Crosby.'

'Aye. I've never seen him back down from a punch-up on the football pitch, man of the cloth or no man of the cloth. But I wouldn't see him generally going looking for a scrap of a Saturday evening. He has to be up for work the next morning of course.'

'I sense a "but" coming.'

'Aye. My faith has not survived well four years of war and some of the shite I've seen and some of the shite I've done. And I've never been overly fond of the clergy to begin with. They deserve to be known as cunts for all eternity for what they did to Parnell.'

'So?'

'So maybe all that leads me to being unfair on the man.

43

But what sort of a man voluntarily swears a vow of celibacy? There is those of us that are celibate through no bleeding choice of our own. And then here is this fucker throws that in our face by taking a public vow that he is never going to have a woman. It's fucking unnatural.'

'Perhaps. But does that make him an abuser and murderer of kids?'

'Maybe not, but it's fucking weird.'

'I can't disagree with you there.'

Eamon dropped the butt of his cigarette into the grass and ground it out with his boot.

'Anyway,' he said, 'let's take it one thing at a time and have a chat with the car owners. Crosby isn't going anywhere fast.'

XI

We walked back to pick up our bikes at the church and then cycled back to McLaughlin's to let him know we were finishing for the day. While we were at it Bronagh did indeed confirm that McLaughlin had been at the office with her at nine o'clock that morning.

Afterwards we set off to visit Dr Hennessy.

Dr Hennessy's home was a big red-brick affair about a quarter of a mile outside town behind a hedge of lime trees and at the end of a decently long drive. It was her husband's but he was killed in France and they had no children. So she was left in it by herself, apart from a girl from the village who came in to clean and cook.

We cycled up to the door and leaned our bikes on the front of the house before we hammered the door knocker.

We waited a while and finally heard a stirring from deep inside the house and a light slowly grew in the glass of the front door. The latch turned and the door swung open revealing Dr Hennessy, in a house coat with her hair glinting coppery from the light of the lamp in her right hand.

'Oh Jesus,' she said. 'Not you fuckers again.'

'Sorry to bother you at this time of night, Doctor, but we need to ask you a few questions. About young Finnegan,' said Eamon.

'Fuck sake,' she said, and let the door swing open wide as she turned to walk back down her hallway, towards her kitchen. We hesitated on the doorstep.

'Education doesn't seem to have noticeably refined this woman's language or hospitality,' Eamon whispered.

'Isn't it just that she is a Dub?'

'Go on so,' said Eamon. I stepped across the threshold followed by Eamon who closed the door behind us, and we headed down the corridor after her.

We found her standing by a large dresser in the kitchen. It was blessedly warm from an iron stove on the far wall. A book was open on her kitchen table with a large glass of wine beside it.

'What are you reading, Doctor?' I asked.

'*War and Peace*,' she said. 'Have you read it?'

'No, but I think Eamon has.'

'Indeed I have,' said Eamon. 'Pierre's a gobshite. Andre is a prick. Natasha is a bit of a floozy. But the battles are good.'

I am not sure which stunned Dr Hennessy more – the fact that Eamon had read any books, let alone this one, or his irreverence. But she composed herself quickly.

'Well, much as I would love to converse on the intricacies of Russian literature, you said you had some questions.'

'You have a car?'

'Indeed I do.'

'Where is it right now?'

'In the garage.'

'Are you sure?'

'Well, it was sitting there half an hour ago when I walked past it.'

'Have you lent it to anyone recently?'

'No. Why do you ask?'

'We found where Liam was put in the water. There were tyre tracks. Hence we deduced his killer was in possession of a pneumatically tyred vehicle.'

'And you thought that I might have strangled and sexually assaulted the child I helped you identify as being murdered.'

'Not really. But we wondered if your car had been used by any others.'

She sighed. 'Sit down for fuck sake,' she said. We did as instructed and she opened the dresser she had been leaning gently against. She took out two more wine glasses and collected an open bottle of red wine from beside the kitchen sink. She sat down and filled the glasses and then raised her own.

'Chin chin,' she said.

'Slainte,' said Eamon.

'Cheers,' I said.

We drank. It was not the first time I had ever had wine, but it wasn't the tenth either. It was nicer than some of the rot-gut I'd had in the past, but I am afraid I had no more imaginative reaction than, 'This isn't bad.'

Eamon was, however, considerably more enthusiastic. 'This is a damned fine wine,' he said. 'I haven't had anything as nice since I left France.'

'My husband was many things, including quite well off. He stocked up the cellar some years ago to guard against such eventualities as uprisings of an ungrateful peasantry interrupting our supply.'

'Sounds like he was a very wise man,' Eamon said. 'Here's to him so,' and we drank again.

'For Keystone Cops, you boys seem to be taking Liam's death a bit seriously.'

'Nothing else to do, Doctor,' said Eamon.

She grunted a laugh.

'So what else have you found out?' she asked.

'Last time he was seen alive was serving Mass on the morning of his death. He left the church at about eight-thirty,' said Eamon.

'And somebody with a car put him in the water,' I added.

'That could have been anyone.'

'Aye. But we are working on the supposition, based on something Mick thinks he read somewhere, that the person who killed him probably knew him.'

'So the person who killed him was someone from the village who had access to one of the cars.'

'Of which, apart from yours, there are five... Well, four and a van.'

Dr Hennessy stuck her hand into her house coat and pulled out a cigarette case and a box of matches. 'Cigarette?' she offered.

Eamon reached for the case and took one. Dr Hennessy lit her own cigarette and then threw the box of matches to Eamon who followed suit. 'Don't you smoke?' she asked.

'I tried one once but it made my head spin and the thought of all that shite in the smoke going into your lungs doesn't seem healthy to me.'

'No more unhealthy than a turf fire,' Eamon said.

'Maybe,' I said, 'but I prefer those with a working chimney.'

Eamon was leaning back in his chair happily sucking in the smoke. 'Now, Doctor,' he said, 'I took you for a woman with more refined taste than Irish fags like these. Something French or Turkish, I would have thought.'

'It's difficult to get such luxuries with you boys rampaging across the country, cutting bridges and blowing up trains and the like. I'm afraid my husband didn't anticipate such depredations being visited upon us.'

'Ach well,' said Eamon, 'even the wisest man is not perfect. And war is hell.'

'William Tecumseh Sherman,' Sophia said.

'Indeed,' said Eamon. 'Remarks to a graduating class at West Point, I believe.'

'He also said,' added Sophia, '"War is cruelty, and you cannot refine it; and those who brought war into our country deserve all the curses and maledictions a people can pour out."'

'We didn't bring this war on our country.'

'Perhaps not. But maybe if you refused to fight, those who did would have to take pause.'

'We've been taking pause for over three hundred years. I'm not sure anyone contemplating the famine graves would argue that has done us much good.'

'Aye, people always find good reasons for killing. If only folk could be comparably compelled towards social justice,' she said.

I said, 'The British presence in our country has been the biggest barrier to social justice. That's true right across the world. It's what Casement said before they hanged him: "when men must beg with bated breath for leave to subsist in their own land, to think their own thoughts, to sing their own songs … then surely it is a braver, a saner, and a truer thing to be a rebel in act and deed against such circumstances as this than tamely to accept it as the natural lot of men."'

'You took the time to learn all that by heart?'

I felt myself blushing. 'I've been short of books for the past couple of weeks. You have to find different ways to occupy your time.'

'No need to explain,' she said. 'Just so long as it makes you feel a bit better about playing cowboys.'

'We are soldiers,' Eamon said. 'Just like your husband was.'

'Aye. And all the good that did him or me.'

'I didn't know your husband and I don't know why he joined up,' said Eamon. 'But me? I joined the Irish Volunteers to secure Home Rule and the chance to make a country where starvation was no more. And when the war came we were told by Redmond and the other leaders of the Irish

49

Parliamentary Party that the best way to secure it would be to fight alongside Britain for Belgium and other small nations just like Ireland. Jaysus I was such a young gobshite to believe that oul shite.'

'And now you are an older gobshite believing different shite?'

'It's difficult for a man with my background in the British Army to be a neutral if I still want to live here.'

'So you align yourself with murderers.'

'Come now, Doctor. You can't believe that the Crown forces are all sweetness and light? Have you not been paying attention to the shenanigans of the Black and Tans of late?'

'So that's the best you can do? Say you're no worse than a horde of mercenaries rampaging in someone else's country?'

'We're not rampaging in someone else's country. We're in our own country. And war is not a game of Tiddlywinks. There has never been one fought without atrocities on all sides.'

'I'd rather it wasn't being done in my name, though.'

'Aye,' said Eamon. 'You're not alone in that aspiration. But probably the last hope of that path died with Parnell.'

They smoked in silence for a moment, and I sipped my wine. Then she turned to me.

'So what sort of gobshite are you?'

I have always had a thing for green eyes. And I was only twenty-two at the time. So when she fixed me with that gaze of hers, it knocked the breath right out of me.

'What do you mean?' I finally managed to stammer out.

'You aren't from Mayo. You aren't even from Connaught. What brings you to these parts with a gun in your hand?'

'I don't actually have a gun.'

'I was speaking metaphorically.'

'I became involved with the anti-conscription protests at university in Galway in 1917. Then at the beginning of October just past the police raided my digs. I'd been on the tear with some classmates, celebrating the start of term, and had crashed out in their place, so I wasn't home when that happened and I avoided the swoop. But it was clear that I couldn't stick around Galway any longer. Or go home. A friend in the movement, Tom Bonner, sent me to his family here. Said they would probably be able to put me up in return for some work about the place, or sort me out with neighbours. They've been very good to me and put me up and I help with the milking in the morning. I thought I should also try to make myself useful to the movement while I was here, so I reported to Commandant O'Riordain and he put me on police duties.'

'What were you studying again?'

'Law.'

'It must be nice you having the chance to see the sort of work Mr McLaughlin gets to do then? See what the future has in store for you, eh? A lifetime of conveyancing and contracts.'

I am still not sure if she was mocking me. 'Actually, I want to be a barrister, not a solicitor. I particularly enjoyed criminal law and was meant to be starting studying evidence this term.'

'Surely Dublin would have been a better place for you than Galway then?'

'It was a concession to my parents. They were worried about Dublin after the Rising. But I liked the idea of Galway as well, and thought it would be a good opportunity to improve my Irish.'

'So how is your Irish?'

'Still shite. But I liked Galway a lot. At least until some-body grassed me up.'

'War is hell,' she said.

'Indeed,' I said.

'Do your family know where you are now?'

'I managed to get word to them shortly after I got here.'

'And how are they?'

'Not too bad. The police showed up looking for me in October, shortly after they raided my digs. But they told them nothing, and the peelers behaved themselves. I think they will lose interest soon enough. They'll have bigger fish to fry.'

'It'll be difficult to have a career in law, let alone at the criminal bar, if you have a criminal record yourself.'

'I suppose we'd better win then.'

Dr Hennessy took a sip of wine as she regarded me over the rim of the glass.

'So what are you doing next?' she asked.

'Interview the other car owners, I suppose. See if they can illuminate matters any further,' said Eamon.

'Hope they let something slip?'

'There is always that hope.'

'Did they teach you anything about criminal investigation in your course, Mick?'

'Not as much as would be useful now.'

She stubbed out her cigarette and stood up lifting the lamp in one hand and her glass of wine in the other. 'Come with me,' she said.

Glasses in hand we followed her out of the kitchen and back up the dark hallway. She stopped halfway and opened a door. We followed her into a room with a large dormer window and with books, floor to ceiling, lining the other three walls. There was a desk and a leather armchair with its back to the window.

She set the lamp down on the desk and picked up a folder. 'I wrote up my notes on the post-mortem examination of Liam. Here, in case it is of some help.'

'Many thanks, Doctor,' said Eamon taking them from her and placing them carefully in his satchel.

'And, if you are short of reading material, Mick, do you want to borrow something?'

'What have you got?'

'Have you ever read Sherlock Holmes?'

'No.'

'Well, there are a couple of collections of Sherlock Holmes stories on the shelves there. I think you might like them.'

I've never turned up my nose at an offer of books, even just a loan. So I followed her directions to the appropriate shelves, and tucked two of them into my knapsack.

'Many thanks, Doctor,' I said.

'Well, it's been nice to chat, but I've got an early morning.'

'Indeed. Thanks, Doctor. We need to be off too,' said Eamon.

We drained the rest of our wine and set the glasses back down on the table in the library. The doctor walked us to the front door. 'Are you going to the funeral tomorrow?'

'We are,' I said.

'Maybe see you there then,' she said and closed the door behind us.

WEDNESDAY

XII

IT WAS A cold clear morning when the village gathered to bury Liam Finnegan.

The church was full and spilling out into the surrounding graveyard. Eamon and I had got there a quarter of an hour before the start of the requiem Mass but had still only managed to get standing room at the back of the church. Peter had gotten there earlier and had managed to get himself a seat in a pew in the middle of the church.

'Okay,' whispered Eamon to me, 'so who do you know here?'

'Dr Hennessy, fourth row back.' She was standing briefly in order to let some people past her into the pew.

'In the short time I have known you, Mick, I have come to admire and respect your capacity for prioritisation. Mind you, she does look good in black, it must be said. Grand arse.'

'Jesus, Eamon, we're at a funeral.'

'A man is most alive when closest to death. You'll find that out in time, Mick. So, who else do you know?'

'There's Mr and Mrs Bonner who I'm staying with up in the second row. And Commandant O'Riordain.'

O'Riordain was in the aisle halfway up the church, trying to create more space amongst the mourners and directing newcomers into the pews.

'There's a man born to lead. Can't even help himself any more.'

'And there's Dick Bruton.' Bruton, who wore a plaid suit, was a fat man with a purple nose. He was bald, which Eamon noted was a blessing for him seeing as he used to be ginger. I'd felt guilty laughing at that as he had always been friendly on the odd occasion I had dropped into his shop, and I felt guiltier now when I saw the bleakly mournful look on the man's face.

'And there, as you should know,' said Eamon, 'is our local neighbourhood cattle baron, Francie Quinn.'

Eamon nodded in the direction of a dark-haired man in a dark suit just entering the church with a pleasant-looking round-faced woman, the sort who you'd normally expect to be smiling, but whose face now seemed washed out with sorrow. Quinn ushered her onto a pew and then found himself standing space against the wall close to her. Quinn, I did know slightly, but I had barely ever spoken to him. He was one of the local worthies that Peter had convinced to join him on the parish court.

Our whispered conversation was halted as the appearance of Paddy Toner, walking backwards up the aisle so he could keep an eye on the pall-bearers and make sure nothing untoward happened to the coffin, announced the arrival of the funeral party.

Normally, in my experience, the deceased would have been carried to the church the night before the burial and lain in vigil before the altar. But the family couldn't bear the thought of leaving Liam alone there. So his body had stayed with them at home until this morning when they would say their final goodbyes.

Liam's father and three uncles followed Toner up the church carrying the tiny coffin on their shoulders. In their wake came the rest of the family. Liam's mother and sister seemed barely able to stand, leaning against each other in an A-frame as they walked up the aisle. Tears were pouring down their faces, though they were considerably quieter now than they had been when we had broken the news to them. Immediately behind them another woman, I presumed an aunt of Liam's though I suppose she might have been a neighbour, carried the baby – I still didn't know his name – who was being remarkably quiet, helped, I presumed, by a bottle of milk stuck in his gob.

When they got to the front of the church Toner ushered the family into the front-row pews that had been reserved for them, and Fr Martin Crosby came on to the altar with four mass-servers in white soutanes.

Crosby was suitably sombre in his conduct of the Mass and proceeded in this measured way until he came to his sermon which he opened with boilerplate remarks about death and young lives cut short that he would have learned in his 'how to conduct a funeral' classes in the seminary. And then his remarks changed and became rather more personal.

'I knew Liam a little from the times he served Mass for me. He was a great young man. A credit to his family. I know he wanted to be a teacher. He was a great reader and used to tell me about what he was reading. The last morning I saw him he was telling me about the adventures of David Balfour after *Kidnapped*. He never lived to find out how it ended with Catriona. He never lived to find his own Catriona or have his own adventures in his own or other lands.

'The world is a lesser place without Liam, without the person he was and without the person he would have become. That truth will never be felt more than by his own family.'

At that, his mother let out the most mournful yelp I've ever heard, and her muffled keening started again.

Crosby continued with the standard funereal hopes that one day all pain would be washed away when they were reunited in heaven. He was trying his best but it was plain that his sermon was doing little to comfort Mrs Finnegan, whose keening died down but whose shoulders continued to shudder in grief until the end of Mass.

XIII

It was a relief to get back out into the fresh air. Even with the onset of winter the unheated church had grown stultifying with so many people in it. I was relieved that, being at the back, we were among the first out after the family and the pall-bearers who carried Liam the final few yards to a hole that had been dug for him in the graveyard that surrounded the church.

O'Riordain had organised a guard of honour of Liam's school friends to walk with the coffin to the gravesite, where

Crosby concluded the service with prayers over the coffin and a decade of the rosary as they lowered Liam into the hole.

The normal routine of friends and neighbours lining up to pay their respects to the family was curtailed as Liam's father led his still weeping wife from the yard. Packy O'Reilly had brought a pony and trap along. As he ushered the sadly depleted Finnegan family on board for the journey back to the farm, the gravediggers began filling in the hole. The earth and stones echoed off the coffin.

'He's not a bad oul skin, Packy,' said Eamon, watching the trap set off as the mass of mourners began to drift out of the graveyard. We leaned against the churchyard wall and Eamon lit a cigarette as we watched folk disperse. Dr Hennessy nodded to us as she passed and began threading her way through the crowd the short distance towards her surgery.

We contemplated the graveyard, Eamon smoking and nodding greetings to friends and neighbours as they passed. Peter joined us after a few minutes.

'You're looking well, Mick,' he said to me. I wasn't sure if he was joking. I was wearing an ill-fitting suit and coat I'd managed to borrow from the Bonners, my fingers barely protruding from the sleeves of the jacket. It was better, I thought, than turning up at a funeral looking like a tramp given the state of my other clothes. But I thought I must have looked absurd. Still I decided to take Peter at his word.

'Thanks,' I said. 'I was trying to show some respect for Liam.'

'Good man,' Peter said.

'Cigarette, Peter?' Eamon asked.

'Thanks, Eamon,' he said and drew one from the packet he was being offered. Eamon struck a match to light him up.

'Sad funeral,' I said.

'Indeed it was,' said Peter. 'No parent should ever have to bury their child, let alone one so young.'

I could see how this funeral must be dragging up memories of Peter's own son, obliterated by a shell in some rat-infested trench in France.

'Have you spoken to his parents?' asked Eamon.

'I have,' said Peter, 'but it's not like there is much comfort I could give them. I told them I know how they feel. I didn't tell them the pain never really goes away or that it can destroy everything you have ever valued in your entire life.'

I remembered how Peter's wife had died shortly after they received news of their son and I had no idea how to respond. I was pretty sure that Eamon was at a loss too. But Peter wasn't looking for sympathy. He was just telling us the truth, as he knew it, of how an untimely and violent death could devastate a family and the lives of all those left behind. Knowing Peter, he was also probably still racking his brain for some fragment of his own experience that could help alleviate the grief and pain of the Finnegans.

We stood in silence for a while, Eamon and Peter smoking, watching the crowd. Francie Quinn hailed Peter as he left the church gate with his wife. Peter waved back. 'He can be a grumpy fecker, can Francie, but he's got a decent soul,' Peter muttered to us as we watched him walking up the street with his wife's hand hooked into his elbow. Then we heard the scrunching of hobnailed boots behind us and Jack

O'Riordain joined us, having come out of the lower gate of the churchyard.

'How's it going, Peter?' he asked, hail-fellow-well-met, even under the grim circumstances.

'Not so bad, Jack. And yourself?'

'Can't complain. Sure no one would listen to me. Are these two behaving themselves?' he asked, referring to me and Eamon.

I expected Peter to make some casual joke, about not being able to get good help these days, or some such. But he didn't. He took a final drag on his cigarette, then dropped it on the footpath and ground it out with his foot. Only then did he look Jack straight in the eye. 'They are exemplary,' he said.

'Glad to hear it,' said Jack. 'I wouldn't want the good name of the battalion damaged by less than their best.'

The children who had attended the funeral were dispersing now too. 'That was a nice idea, the guard of honour,' said Peter.

'I wanted to make sure the children were involved in the funeral, and I thought it was a way we could show Liam's family the regard the whole school held him in.'

'Aye. It was a nice gesture,' said Peter. 'Did you give the kids the day off school as well?'

'I did,' said Jack. 'You can imagine that they are all still very upset. But kids get over such things fast, I've found.'

'You've seen much of this sort of thing, Commandant?' I asked. 'The deaths of children, I mean.'

'Regrettably, yes,' he said. 'Particularly when I was teaching in Dublin. The carnage from tuberculosis was dreadful. The conditions in the tenements there are a breeding ground for

60

disease, and the malnourishment of the children makes them easy prey for it.'

'So, you're at a loose end yourself then today as well?' Peter asked.

'If only that were so. I have a host of battalion matters to be dealing with, as well as some school administration I've been falling behind on.'

Eamon had been quiet up to that point, but I knew he couldn't help himself. 'Some more unarmed peelers to be shot, Jack?' he asked.

I saw anger darken O'Riordain's face and the muscles in his jaw clench.

'For God's sake, Eamon,' said Peter.

'No,' said Jack, his voice low and controlled, irrespective of how angry he was. 'It's sticking in his gut, let him get it out. I imagine that Eamon's military record is unblemished and earns him the right to judge. Isn't that the case, Eamon?'

Eamon said nothing.

'That's right,' said O'Riordain, 'your hands are not so clean either. I remember you telling me about that, didn't you, Eamon? About young Germans crying for their mothers before you and your British pals put bullets in them and left them in the mud.'

'I wasn't the officer giving orders,' said Eamon.

'No,' said Jack, 'I was. But you can take a little credit for what we did at the barracks.'

'What do you mean?' asked Eamon. 'I refused to participate.'

'You did,' said Jack, 'and loudly too. I never knew you had studied the Hague Conventions so assiduously. That was the

61

point at which I knew you were no use to the battalion any more as a fighting man. But that is not what I meant.'

'What then?'

'The tales you have told me of the Crown forces have left me with little doubt as to their ruthless efficiency. It confirmed what we learned when they shelled the civilian population of Dublin and left the second city of their empire in flames, let alone the savagery they showed at Amritsar and countless other places across their bloody empire. Now look at our lot. Weekend soldiers. In the past year these fellows have had less training than the greenest Tommy. And it is with them that I am meant to confront a portion of that empire. Those police in that barracks were traitors to their country. And their treason cost the lives of James Flynn, John McKenna and Paddy McCaul, remember? It was harsh what I did. But it was necessary. It was necessary to get the rest of the boys used to killing. It was necessary because I thought that it might save their lives in the months to come when next in the presence of the enemy. So when they are in action again they are inoculated to the revulsion of killing, and to not hesitate at the moment of truth. Remember, Eamon?'

He paused and looked at Eamon with something close to contempt.

'I didn't enjoy what I did that night,' said O'Riordain. 'I will have to live with the sound of their pleading every day until I die. But I would do it again, for the good of the men under my command and for the chance of a country of our own.'

We were all quiet. 'Anything else to say, Volunteer Gleason?'

'No, Commandant,' said Eamon.

'Okay so,' said O'Riordain. 'I'll be on my way then. And you've work to do too, so don't let Mr McLaughlin down the way you did me.' He turned to Peter. 'Take care of yourself, Peter,' he said and shook his hand. Then to us, 'Volunteers,' and he turned up the street.

'Commandant,' I said by way of farewell. Eamon said nothing.

We watched O'Riordain go. Then Peter turned to Eamon, 'For God's sake, Eamon,' he said. 'Do you always have to antagonise him?' Peter was more exasperated than angry, but only just.

Eamon was uncharacteristically quiet and looked a bit shame-faced. 'We have a bit of history, I suppose,' he said eventually.

'Well, it's not particularly helpful at the moment, so can you get it under control?'

'I can,' said Eamon.

'Look, boys,' said Peter, 'I meant it when I said ye've been exemplary in your duties to the parish court. So don't make a liar of me at this stage in my life.'

'We won't, Peter. Sorry if I've embarrassed you,' said Eamon.

'That's enough of that oul shite,' said Peter. 'Now I've given ye an enquiry to conduct, which, I shouldn't need to remind you, is of the most sensitive nature imaginable, so tread lightly from here on, will ye?'

'We will,' said Eamon.

'Good. Now I need to be getting back to the office, so can I leave ye to be getting on with it without fecking something else up?'

'You can,' said Eamon.

'Good. I'll leave ye to it, so, and I'll see ye later.'

'Right, Peter,' said Eamon.

'Take care,' I said.

He said nothing and turned and walked up the street towards his office. We watched him as he went, his shoulders hunched in the way of the worried, carrying the burdens of the world.

There were a few remaining knots of people still chatting or smoking in the graveyard or on the street, but most had gone back to the normal routine of their lives. Myself and Eamon remained by the churchyard wall until everyone had left, Eamon brooding over the scene as he smoked another cigarette.

'That was kind of Peter, speaking up for us with O'Riordain,' I said.

''Twas,' said Eamon. 'He's like that, is Peter. Always championing the underdog. It's why he loses so much money on the horses.'

In spite of the lambasting he had just taken I could sense that Eamon's spirit was returning. 'Did you hear that fucker, O'Riordain?' he asked. '"Can't complain, sure no one would listen." Anyone not paying attention to O'Riordain's little gripes would run a serious risk of getting plugged in the nut.'

I grunted a laugh. I might have laughed more but the thought that O'Riordain had been contemplating, however vaguely, putting a bullet at the base of my skull took most of the humour out of it.

'So what now?' I said as Eamon crushed the butt of his fag into the ground.

'Let's have a chat to Dick Bruton about his car, I suppose.'

XIV

Bruton had just settled his substantial arse on a stool behind the cash register of his general store when we arrived. He had a mug of tea beside him and was in the process of opening a copy of a newspaper when he caught sight of us.

'Gentlemen!' he said.

'How's it going, Dick?' said Eamon.

'Can't complain,' said Bruton, 'sure no one would listen to me.'

'Sad funeral.'

'Indeed it was. Sure we all have to go sometime, but you hope for a long life and to die surrounded by those you love. Liam had all his life before him.'

'Aye,' said Eamon, and we all fell silent for a moment.

'Well, how can I help you boys?' asked Bruton.

'A pound of ham, cut thick, half a pound of butter, and a wheaten loaf,' I said. The Bonners were very good to me and kept me fed, but only just. Fortunately, the small salary I drew as a full-time member of the Republican Police allowed me to supplement what they gave me.

Bruton slid his arse off his stool and walked over to the butcher's counter.

'Just yourself today, Dick?' Eamon asked.

'It is,' he said. 'The wife will be in a bit later but she's off making the dinner at the moment. The two girls who work here are off today. They are still very upset about Liam.'

'Young Liam used to work here, I understand?'

'He did. Saturdays only. And the holidays. Packing bags, stacking shelves, helping with deliveries.'

'What was he like?' I asked.

'You heard Father Crosby. A bright young fella. A hard worker. A bit awkward in himself. Roisin and Collette, the girls that work here, used to tease him a bit and he was easily embarrassed. Reminded me of myself at that age, and all through my teens, for that matter. Very shy with the girls. I should have stopped them messing with the young fella, but they meant no harm. They liked him, in fact, and I thought that sort of thing never did me any harm. He needed to get through it, like. I'm sorry about that now.'

'Well, you couldn't have known he was never going to see the other side of that awkward phase,' said Eamon.

'No. But I should have been kinder.'

'When was the last time you saw him?'

'Saturday. He was here from half past nine until closing time.'

'Six?'

'Aye, six. He'd normally stay till seven and help clean up, but he had a load of shopping for his ma and I sent him home a bit early. The weather was looking as if it might break.'

'That was kind of you so,' I said.

For a moment I thought Bruton was going to cry. But he pulled a handkerchief out of his pocket and made a show of coughing into it. It gave him time to compose himself.

'Sorry, what else was it you said you wanted?' Bruton had finished slicing and wrapping the ham as he spoke to us.

'Half a pound of butter and a loaf of wheaten bread,' I said. He gathered those together and placed them with the ham into a brown paper bag. I paid him with a ten-shilling note.

'You need anything, Eamon?' Bruton asked.

'No groceries, thanks, Dick. But I do have a bit of police business.'

'How can I help you, Eamon?'

'Has anybody spoken to you before about your trading with the enemies of the Republic?'

Bruton blanched and swallowed audibly.

'That's a guilty reaction,' said Eamon.

'What do you mean?' asked Bruton.

'You continued supplying the police barracks with food and drink for weeks after the legitimate representatives of the Republic instructed you to stop.'

Bruton sat down on his stool and tried to control his breathing.

'Jesus, Eamon. A man has to feed his family.'

'You'd be supplying them still if we hadn't put the barracks out of business.'

'Jesus, no. Sure you know I'm a supporter of the Republic. I'm the biggest contributor to the National Loan in these parts.'

'It's that that gets you the courtesy visit, Dick. There's hard days ahead when good neighbourliness might have to come to an end.'

'But I'm on your side, boys. What else can I do to prove it?'

Eamon was quiet for a moment.

'We may have to call on you for logistical support in the not-too-distant future.'

'Logistical what?'

'Logistics: the activity of organising the movement, equipment, supplies and accommodation of troops.'

'Oh,' said Bruton.

'Is your van still in running order?'

'It is.'

'When was the last time you had it out?'

'Monday. I went over to Castlebar to the wholesalers, to stock up.'

'About what time?'

'I left early, about half past eight.'

'Van running okay?'

'Aye, grand.'

'What time did you get back?'

'Late afternoon.'

'A sort of a leisurely excursion for you then?'

'Not really. I had my lunch in the hotel. Thought I'd treat myself. But it's a longer trip now since Jack cut the main road to there.'

O'Riordain had put trenches across the main road to Castlebar, which held one of the few remaining British garrisons in Mayo. He did it the day after he had taken the barracks to discourage any counterattack by the Crown forces up that road. The trenches were watched over by teams of three Volunteers, rotated regularly and armed with two of the battalion's few Lee-Enfield rifles, to delay the British with sniping and to get word back to town if they ever tried to repair the trenches and storm into town on their Crossley tenders. Eamon had judged it a sensible measure but confessed that he would feel better about it if he believed that O'Riordain also properly understood the concept of flanking movements and was keeping a proper eye on the other routes into town, which Eamon felt were being patrolled only haphazardly.

'Anything unusual about the trip?'

'Nothing, really. I mean, the police stopped me at the edge of Castlebar and searched the van. Same going out. But apart from that, nothing.'

'Did they ask you any questions?'

'Just the usual. My name. Where I'd come from.'

'You didn't volunteer anything else to them, did you, Dick?'

'Jesus no, Eamon. No fucking way on God's green earth.'

'Make sure and keep it that way, Dick. We've had enough funerals in these parts for a while,' said Eamon.

Eamon turned, and I followed him out the shop. As I stepped through the door I turned for a moment to look at Bruton. He had his tea halfway to his mouth and was spilling its contents across his vest.

XV

Finally we were sitting alone again in the snug at the back of Toner's, with two pints of Guinness, a plate of ham sandwiches, a butter knife and the detritus of the shopping between us.

'So what are you thinking, Mick?'

'Did you mean to scare the shite out of Bruton?'

'Not really. But when I saw that I had unnerved him, I thought it probably useful if he stayed scared. Make him a bit more cooperative.'

'It was a bit cruel.'

'He was keeping the police barracks supplied when he was told not to. O'Riordain would likely be much crueller if Dick doesn't mend his ways.'

'O'Riordain doesn't already know?' I asked.

'I saw no reason to tell Jack. Though frankly, if anyone less of a complete fucking eejit than Shamey O'Neill was battalion intelligence officer, poor Dick would probably be keeping those peelers company behind the barracks. Still, putting that barracks out of business when we did probably saved Dick's life. Even a fecking gobshite as stupid as Shamey is going to blunder into some actual intelligence sooner or later.'

'Bruton was out in his car on Monday morning.'

'Indeed. And the back road to Castlebar passes both the church, the school and the point at the river where we think Liam went into the water. And the back of that van is roomy. Plenty of space to fuck a youngster in if you were of that sort of mind.'

'But can you see that man having the guts to harm a fly let alone a youngster?'

'It does stretch the imagination. But it's one thing getting confronted by the IRA – well, IRP in our case. It's another thing altogether when you are the one with power over some-one weaker.'

'Did you spend your spare time in the trenches reading Freud or Jung?'

'Not so much. But I have seen fuckers who shite them-selves in a barrage beating and raping young girls. So I'm not convinced that courage is necessarily a prerequisite for cruelty or murder.'

'Did you see many such fuckers?'

'To be fair just the one. But I've heard plenty of stories of others.'

'What happened to your one?'

'He walked into a bullet during an action a few weeks later.'

'A German bullet?'

'Fuck off,' said Eamon.

'And the girl?'

'She was a prostitute. After she got out of hospital I understand she returned to her professional duties. Not like there were very many other options in those parts if you didn't want to starve to death.'

I thought about pressing Eamon for some more details of this story but decided against it. So instead I said, 'But Bruton seems like a decent soul. Not the sort who would generally be raping or abusing children or young prostitutes.'

'That fucker in France seemed like a decent soul too at the beginning. Some things you never really know until that moment of truth.' Eamon took a pull on his pint. 'So what do you think of Crosby?' he asked.

'I'm thinking that sermon didn't sound like the words of a child murderer.'

'You are basing this on the conversations you have had with all the other child murderers?'

'I'm basing this on my inference from his sermon that he felt Liam's death keenly and was grieving himself.'

'Aye,' said Eamon, 'he certainly gave that impression. Bruton looked as if he was tearing up a bit too. But I'm thinking if he was a sick enough fucker to fiddle with a youngster and then murder him to stop getting found out, then he might not be the sort of fellow who would have trouble with a few crocodile tears over the corpse of said youngster. And there is plenty of space and quiet in a church vestry to do all sorts.'

'Indeed,' I said. 'But for now this is all just conjecture and supposition. We have no evidence that Bruton is a child abuser, let alone a murderer. The same goes for Crosby.'

'You've read about the Borgias, Mick? Some of them popes were randy fuckers. Why should a parish priest be any different?'

'Rodrigo Borgia was mostly into adult and generally willing women, I thought, though he wasn't above putting on a tableau of young men and courtesans copulating as dinner party entertainment for his wealthy guests.'

'There was all sorts of sexual perversity going on amongst them fuckers. All sorts of shite going on throughout the institutional church for centuries. Why do we think today is any different? It's the same old story. Power. Abuse of power. Cardinal Cesare Borgia spent weeks raping – what was the name of that duchess whose cities he captured?'

'Caterina?'

'Caterina! That's right. Spent weeks raping her after he sacked her cities. And then the conscienceless little bastard consigned her to the dungeons once he tired of her. Those with power and impunity always make a point of having and enjoying what they think are their just deserts. And Crosby is a big fish around here. He likes to do the man-of-the-people thing. But ninety per cent of the parish treat him like royalty, and the other ten per cent is Protestant. And that has been his life for the past twenty years. Must make him a bit notionous. Must make him think maybe he is entitled to a bit of leeway from the precise strictures of the canon law from time to time.'

'It's still a big jump to murder.'

'Maybe.'

'And I don't think Cesare was a cardinal any more when he embarked on his military career.'

'Ah! Another student of the Borgias. Well then, you'll already know that first his da sorted him out with the red hat to make him a prince of the church, and then when that didn't suit the needy little bastard he set him up as a prince temporal instead. It must be nice to have your da the pope.'

'You may have avoided Freud but you still appear to have done a hell of a lot of reading in them trenches. When did you ever get time to shoot anyone?'

'Take my word for it: there was plenty of time for that too.'

We took a sup of our pints.

'What did your da do?' I asked.

'Blacksmith. Yours?'

'Farmer.'

'Beef?'

'Pigs.'

'Well, we've a cattle man to see yet. So anything you have picked up from the Bonners might come in useful for the chat.'

'I just about know how to milk a cow now, so I'm not sure that will be much help.'

'Well, it's more than I know about cows.'

'Will we go see him now?' I asked.

'It's Wednesday, so he'll have gone to the mart in Ballina after the funeral, and probably on the batter after that. So we'll need to wait until tomorrow. With luck he'll still have a hangover. Might make him testy and a bit looser with his words.'

'So what do we do until then?'

'Well, first of all we'll have a game of chess. And then you can fuck off and read some of that Sherlock Holmes. See if it gives you any ideas.'

XVI

It was past six when I left Eamon rereading Dr Hennessy's medical report on Liam and negotiated my way through the throng of Toner's public bar to the fresh air of the street.

Shamey O'Neill was sitting with a small group of Volunteers I didn't know close to the bar. He stopped talking and eyed me suspiciously as I squeezed through the crowd. Out of habit, and perhaps the hope of mending some fences, I nodded greetings to him as I passed. He didn't acknowledge me. He just kept looking. I'm sure his eyes were following me as I left.

The street was empty and it was already dark. The pavement was wet from a shower of rain that had been and gone. I lifted my bicycle from the wall but was feeling a bit unsteady so I decided to walk with it a little before mounting up.

I saw Dr Hennessy coming out of her surgery on the other side of the street and bending to lock the door after she closed it. 'Evening, Doctor,' I said.

She looked up. 'Oh. Mick,' she said. 'What's the craic?'

'Not too bad,' I said, 'all things considering.'

'I saw you at the funeral,' she said. 'God, it was very sad. I thought at one point even Father Crosby was going to start crying.'

'At one point I felt I was even going to start crying and I didn't even know the young fella.'

'It's terrible for the family.'

'It must be. I can only imagine.'

'Anything to report from your… investigations?' She hesitated like she was coming to terms with the absurdity of us two bogmen trying to emulate the detectives of Dublin Castle or Scotland Yard.

'Nothing really, just taking one thing at a time and trying to piece it together.'

'Still working your way through car owners.'

'Aye,' I said, 'that and Sherlock Holmes.'

She smiled. 'What do you make of him?'

'He's a bit of an arsehole, isn't he? But the puzzles are compelling. Keeps you reading.'

'Aye, that's what I thought too. He never ceases to be anything but an arsehole. But it's enjoyable reading.'

''Tis indeed,' I said. 'How are you getting on with *War and Peace*?'

'Your pal Eamon was right. Pierre is a bit of a gobshite.'

'Has Bonaparte shown up yet?'

'He's just won at Austerlitz. Eamon was right about that too. The battles are good.'

She pushed the surgery keys into her handbag and then rummaged around a bit more until she retrieved another set.

'Well, I don't mean to be rude,' she said, 'but I've got a house call to make before I get my dinner, so I'd best be on my way.' She moved towards her car which was parked beside the kerb. 'Whenever you have finished with Holmes and Watson let me know. As you have seen, I have quite an extensive library. Might get you started with a little bit of Chekhov next.'

'That's very kind of you, Doctor.'

'Not at all. Always good to have a few more people about with an interest in literature.'

She stepped into her car and started the engine. 'It was lovely to see you, Mick. Take care and have a good evening.' She smiled and waved to me as she drove off.

'Jesus,' I thought as I waved back, 'she must be a witch,' and I remembered those stories my da used to tell me in the darkness by the fireside at Halloween, about green-eyed women who would steal your heart away and replace it with a stone.

THURSDAY

XVII

WE KNOCKED ON Francie Quinn's door at nine the next morning.

His wife, the pleasant-looking woman with the round face who we had seen at the funeral, answered the door.

'Is your husband about?' asked Eamon.

'He is,' she said. 'He's just finished his breakfast.'

She led us into the parlour where Quinn was sitting at a desk. He appeared to be going over account books.

'Will ye have a cup of tea?' Mrs Quinn asked us.

'That's very kind of you. We will,' said Eamon and planted himself on a chair across the desk from Quinn. I followed suit and sat down too.

'What's the craic, boys?' asked Francie once his wife had left for the kitchen.

'We just have a few questions regarding your whereabouts on Monday.'

'Why? What am I meant to have done?'

'Ach, the way it is now, Francie, is that we'll do the asking of the questions, what with us being the Republican Police and all.'

Quinn didn't look amused. I don't suppose he was used to people giving him cheek, and from what Eamon said, in the days of yore when cheek had been given to him he had been known to be short with his temper and fast with his fists. I wondered if marriage had mellowed him. Certainly, his standing in the community had risen with his wealth over the years to such an extent that Peter had recruited him, along with a farmer called Barney O'Hara, to join him on the parish court. Though the achievement of having established a functional court had probably not completely assuaged McLaughlin's disappointment at not recruiting Crosby. The presence of a priest on the court would certainly have added considerably to its respectability in the eyes of his parishioners.

It occurred to me that perhaps, given his presence on the court now, Quinn may have regarded us as cheeky subordinates, showing up at his house with questions. Still, he humoured us with an answer.

'I was here till about lunchtime and then I went into the village with the wife to Bruton's to do some shopping.'

'Anyone vouch for that?'

'Ciara, my wife, was here all morning with me.'

'Even when you were out doing the milking?' I asked.

'I have Packy O'Reilly to do the milking.'

'Did Packy see you?'

'Only in the early afternoon, when he came in looking for a rope.'

'Ah,' said Eamon. 'Did he say why he wanted a rope?'

'No. He did seem a bit flustered but I'm afraid I didn't give that much thought at the time.'

'So who else did you see on Monday?'

'That girl, whatever her name is, the one that works in Bruton's shop.'

'Not his wife.'

'No, the young one with the black hair. Bruton was off in Castlebar, she told me. And I saw your Commandant, Jack O'Riordain, on the road.'

'Did you speak to him?'

'Briefly.'

'What about?'

'Mind your own fucking business.' Francie's shallow reservoir of good humour had run dry.

Eamon kept his cool. 'May I remind you that we are here on official Republican Police business?'

'So you say. But if it is so important I am somewhat surprised that Peter has not briefed me on it. So I'm not going to divulge sensitive information to any Tom, Dick or gobshite who comes through my door unannounced and uninvited. Does Peter even know you are here?'

'Mr McLaughlin has instructed us to look into some sensitive matters for him. We have not had time to appraise him on the precise details of our enquiries to date,' I said.

'Well, if you want to find out more about my dealings with Commandant O'Riordain you had best speak to Jack for yourselves, if you have the balls.'

It was, I think, the first time I had seen Eamon unsettled.

Just then Mrs Quinn came through the door carrying the tea on a tray. She sensed the awkwardness but set down the tray on her husband's desk and cheerfully declared, 'Enough of that now, boys. Have a cup of tea and no more angry words.'

I gingerly reached over and picked up a cup while Quinn continued to glower at Eamon. Mrs Quinn walked around the desk and stood beside her husband placing her hands on his shoulders. He didn't react. 'Come on, Francie. Drink your tea now,' and she nudged his side playfully with her arse.

That seemed to calm him a bit and he reached for the tea.

'It's you we have to thank for the rope we used to get young Liam Finnegan out of the river,' I said.

'No thanks are required. I'd much prefer the rope hadn't been needed at all.'

'Did you lend Packy the horse and trap to give the Finnegans a lift back from the church too?'

'It was the least I could do for neighbours,' he said.

We fell into an awkward silence again for a moment, but Mrs Quinn wasn't having it.

'So you are the mysterious man from the north we've been hearing about,' she said to me.

'I am,' I said.

'First time in the west?'

'Ah no, I was studying in Galway for the past couple of years. But it's my first time to Mayo.'

'How are you finding us?'

'Well, I wish I was here under different circumstances. But the hospitality of the people compensates for the hostility of the climate.'

'Oh, 'tis a charmer you are, isn't that right, Francie?'

Quinn grunted. Eamon swallowed his tea and stood up. 'Many thanks for your time and your tea, Mrs Quinn, but I fear we must be on our way. If I may trouble you with one more question, Mr Quinn?' – not 'Francie' any more.

'What is it?'

'When you saw Commandant O'Riordain was he on foot?'

'No, he was in his car.'

'Many thanks again for your time.'

I stood also and Mrs Quinn showed us to the door, bidding us farewell as if we were favoured relatives rather than the unwelcome upstart police her husband plainly saw us as.

We walked our bikes together to the gate of the Quinn property.

'Jesus,' I said. 'We poked a bear with a sore head there.'

Eamon said nothing, but leaned his bike against the gatepost and lit a cigarette.

'Something unsettled you in there,' I said.

'Aye,' said Eamon, 'you could certainly put it like that,'

'What is it?'

'Quinn implied he's having dealings with the IRA, which was news to me. So Jack is keeping it quiet or at least keeping it quiet from us. If I'd known that I'd have approached that conversation rather differently.'

'Why?'

'Because asking about stuff that you aren't meant to know about is a very bad habit. Particularly when the IRA commandant already hates your fucking guts.'

'What do you think they might be up to together?'

'Could be anything. Running guns. Financing the battalion. General logistics.'

'What do you think we should do? Speak to O'Riordain?'

'Because the last conversation I had with Jack went so well?'

'You think he holds a grudge?'

'I know he holds a grudge. But that's not what bothers me. What bothers me is that he holds a grudge at the head of a small army, with licence to do much as he pleases in these parts.'

Not for the first time I wished I was back home in front of the fire listening to my da talking about the farm and the neighbours. I wished I was bored and safe amongst people I loved, rather than here, on the edge of Ireland, amongst strangers, half of whom seemed suspicious of me just on the basis of my accent.

Eamon dropped his cigarette on the road and ground it out. 'Okay,' he said. 'Let's get a move on.'

XVIII

We cycled up to the church and leaned our bicycles against the wall of the adjacent parochial house. We rapped on the door, and Crosby answered it himself. He didn't have a housekeeper, which, as far as Eamon was concerned, was further evidence of a particularly fishy stench about the reverend father.

'What do you boys want this time?' Crosby asked.

'A few minutes of your time, if we may, Father,' said Eamon. Crosby let the door fall open and we followed him in.

He paused at the doorway to his parlour and turned to us. 'Do youse want a cup of tea?' he asked.

Eamon answered for both of us. 'No,' he said. 'Just a conversation.'

Crosby led us into the room. He sat down on a leather armchair and we took up position on a sofa across from him. It was a nice room, clean and neat, with the fire burning in the hearth flanked by two well-populated bookcases, and a low table in the middle. There was a book open on the table. From where I was sitting I couldn't make out the title or subject matter.

'This is the closest I've seen you to a church, Eamon, since you came back from France,' Crosby said, friendly enough, I suppose. But neither of us smiled. 'So what is it you want then?' he asked.

'How's your car running?' asked Eamon.

'It's running fine, thanks,' said Crosby. 'I don't use it so much at the moment, what with the price of petrol and the state of the roads. Only if the weather is bad, or when I have to run into Ballina or Castlebar. Why do you ask?'

'Were you out on Monday?'

'I was. I went over to Castlebar.'

'What time did you leave?'

'About nine.'

'And when did you get back?'

'About half twelve.'

'Anybody see you on the way?'

'No idea. But I bumped into Dick Bruton when I was there. He was on his way to the hotel, he told me, for his lunch. Asked me if I wanted to join him.'

'Did you?'

'No.'

'Why not?'

'It was meant to be my day off. I didn't fancy sitting listening to the groans and gripes of parishioners.'

'Not very Christian of you.'

'I'm a priest, not a saint. And with the main road being cut now I knew it was going to take me a while to get back, so I really didn't want to dawdle,' said Crosby.

'Did you see any police on your way?'

'There was an army road block on the entry to Castlebar, but they waved me through when they saw my dog collar.'

'And they didn't stop you on your way back home either?'

'No.'

'So what took you to Castlebar in the first place?'

'I had a bit of shopping to do.'

'Bruton's store not good enough for you?'

'I needed some clothes, and I wanted to go to the library.'

'Run out of black pyjamas, did you, Father?' asked Eamon.

'Aye,' said Crosby, 'there's a joke I have not heard at least once a week for the past twenty years.'

I thought it might be useful to be a bit more conciliatory so I asked, 'What are you reading at the moment?'

'Nothing serious. Some cowboy stories. Once more, can I ask what this is about?'

'It's like this, Father. Liam Finnegan didn't die accidentally. He was murdered.'

Crosby hesitated for a moment before asking, 'What makes you think that?'

'Now that's an interesting question,' said Eamon.

'Why so?'

'Because it's not what I would have expected you to say when being told that a child you had known, one you evinced grief over, had been murdered.'

Crosby opened his mouth but nothing came out.

'I suppose there is two ways you could have known. Someone could have told you in confession,' said Eamon. Crosby said nothing.

'Or you could have done it yourself?'

'Fuck,' said Crosby.

'Yes,' said Eamon. 'He was fucked as well, before he died.'

Crosby opened his mouth and closed it again. We waited. Finally he spoke. 'Dr Hennessy told me about it.'

I'm not sure what we had been expecting to hear from him but it certainly hadn't been that.

'When?' I asked.

'On Monday. After she had conducted the post-mortem. She came round here after for a cup of tea. She was upset.'

'I suspected as much,' said Eamon.

'How? Why?' I asked.

'Keystone Cops,' said Eamon.

'What?' asked Crosby.

'On Tuesday evening she called us the Keystone Cops. Like you did on Tuesday afternoon. I also thought it was a bit of a coincidence that she lent young Mick here the collected tales of Holmes and Watson, which was another of your witty allusions to our duties here.'

Crosby said nothing. 'Just a cup of tea, was it, Father?' asked Eamon.

'Just a cup of tea.'

'So you're particularly friendly with the Doc, are you, Father?'

'I've got to know her well over the past couple of years. We both tend to show up on the worst day of people's lives.'

'And you are close enough that she trusts you with privileged information?'

'It would seem so, wouldn't it? It is, after all, part of my job.'

'Well, Father, I'm afraid we are not so trusting. So far as we can ascertain you were the last person to see Liam alive. So you had the opportunity. You have a cock and two hands, so you had the means. We believe he was put into the river from a vehicle with pneumatic tyres, something that you are in possession of. The road to Castlebar passes close to where he was put in the water. And frankly you were a bit shifty on Tuesday when we spoke to you, so you either have some more explaining to do, or perhaps we'll take this matter up with the bishop.'

Crosby snorted at that. 'No offence, lads, but even if the bishop believed a couple of shite hawks like youse, don't you think his aversion to scandal would lead him to use his influence to keep things a bit quiet?'

'Ah, the persistent arrogance of the clergy,' said Eamon. 'Be that as it may you still have a bit of explaining to do.'

'Like what?'

'You mentioned that you offered Liam a cup of tea on Monday morning, after Mass.'

'What of it?'

86

'Are you in the habit of doling out tea to the altar boys?'

'It was a cold morning. He looked like he could do with some warming up.'

'Bit of wine, I always find, warms them up faster. You weren't tempted to dig into the sacristy stockpile?'

'For fuck sake,' said Crosby.

'Try and look at it from our perspective, Father. Both myself and Mick here served Mass for more years than we care to remember. Neither of us were ever offered a cup of tea by any priest.'

'Maybe it's just because you were both cunts.'

'Lovely language for a priest, eh, Mick?'

'The shite you boys have brought to my door would wring worse language from less reasonable people.'

'To be fair,' I said, 'it was good enough for Shakespeare.'

'Indeed,' said Eamon. '*Hamlet*, wasn't it?'

'It was,' I said.

'Which is appropriate because we are discussing a case of "murder most foul" here too. And, as far as I am concerned, Father Crosby, you had opportunity, means and motive.'

'What, in the name of God, could my motive have been for killing Liam?' asked Crosby.

'Call me prejudiced, Father, but I have always felt that someone who makes so ostentatious a show of celibacy, must be hiding something.'

'It is to allow us to give our whole selves to the church and our parishioners.'

'Hmm,' said Eamon. 'I've heard tell in Belgium and France of prostitutes who specialise in the servicing of the clergy.'

'Priests are human too.'

'Not so many such establishments in these parts. I would reckon that the nearest establishment that might offer a full menu to satisfy this and all such sexual perversities must be as far away as Limerick. You know what them Limerick fuckers are like, almost as West British as the Pale. But you'd have to find your release in other ways.'

'By raping and murdering children?'

'My years in France and Belgium have not enhanced my opinion of the nature of human beings. Even priests. Particularly priests. And you are not making much headway in changing those perceptions.'

'Isn't presumption of innocence something? Or is that going to be done away with too in this new republic that you and your friends are promising us?'

'Presumption of innocence is for McLaughlin and the courts to deal with. Our job is to find out who killed Liam, in order to ensure no other children of this parish are harmed in a similar way.'

'I've told you all I can,' said Crosby.

Eamon stood abruptly and looked down at Crosby. 'This isn't the end of it, Father. We'll be back.'

I followed Eamon out of the house. He had already lit a cigarette and I could tell he was struggling to get his breathing under control.

He looked at me. 'That Crosby's a supercilious fucker and one of these days he's going to get his.'

XIX

The waiting room in Dr Hennessy's surgery had half a dozen people in it, a combination of mothers and children, some of the kids sniffing very loudly. We would as soon have barged straight into Dr Hennessy's examination room to demand answers but Laoise, Dr Hennessy's receptionist, was a fierce one and told us, in no uncertain terms, to put manners on ourselves and not to be interrupting the doctor's private conversations with her patients. We breathed deeply. Sat down. And waited.

After what seemed like an interminable period, the door to the examination room opened to disgorge another mother and child. Eamon was at it before Laoise could say a word.

'We need to speak to you, Doctor.'

'I'm sorry, Doctor,' said Laoise. 'I told them they had to wait.'

'It's all right,' said Dr Hennessy. She didn't give us the same attitude as she had when we visited on Monday. Instead it was a businesslike. 'Come in,' she said.

She sat back behind her desk and asked, 'What can I do for you?'

'Father Martin Crosby.'

'What about him?' she asked.

'I told you not to go blabbing about the findings of your examination on Liam Finnegan. It seems the reverend father was quite fully appraised of our concerns when we spoke to him earlier.'

'Ah,' she said. 'Sorry. I was upset and spoke to him in what I thought was confidence.'

'Some confidences are held lightly when you are accused of murder.'

She looked taken aback for a second. Then burst out laughing. 'You accused Martin Crosby of Liam's murder?'

'We intimated to him that we considered him to be a compelling suspect. He is the owner of a car. His account of his encounter with Liam on Monday morning is problematic and unsupported by other witnesses. In short, he had motive, means and opportunity.'

'What motive?'

'He's a priest. Some of those fellas have bizarre sexual tastes.'

'Based on what? On salacious stories of the Borgias that you have heard down the pub and embellished beyond all recognition of the historical facts?'

Eamon blinked at that, and then let out a deep breath. 'I was married once, Doctor,' he said. This was new information. It gave me a bit of a start.

'That I did not know,' said Dr Hennessy. 'But why is that relevant in any way, shape or form?'

'Bear with me, Doctor. She was a nurse in France.'

'English?'

'No, French. From Paris, of all places.'

'What did she see in a bogman like you?'

'Never quite worked that out myself, Doctor, and too late to ask her now.'

'She found greener pastures.'

'She was killed in a barrage in August 1918, working in a casualty clearing station close to the front lines.'

'Oh,' she said. 'I'm sorry.'

'Not to worry, Doc. We all have our sad stories to tell. Anyway, when I knew her she was a fierce little communist. But she hadn't always been so. Convent school girl and all that. What turned her against the church was the children. Before the war she worked in a poor neighbourhood in Paris, she told me, with two big Catholic schools, one for boys, one for girls. One day a mother brought her pregnant daughter to see her.'

'And the father was a priest.'

'Indeed. But when the girl opened up to Juliette, my wife, it was but the tip of the iceberg. The young schoolgirls dealing with the unwanted attentions of the priests. The young schoolboys dealing with the unwanted attentions of the priests.'

'All of the priests?'

'No, a few notorious ones. But the others covered it up and most of the nuns were not much better.'

'I can assure you, Eamon, that I have dealt with no such scandals in the vicinity of Ballykennedy.'

'Until now.'

'Martin Crosby did not rape and kill Liam.'

'How can you be so sure?'

'I've known him for six years. He was very good to me when my husband died, and I am not even of his faith. And I've seen him dealing with bereavement of all sorts over the years. He may have a brusque manner sometimes, but he is a kind man and a fine priest.'

'Priests are human too. And all human beings have their dark side.'

'That is a particularly pitch-black shade of darkness, and I simply don't see it in him.'

'Are you willing to bet your life on that? More to the point, are you willing to bet the lives of the children you are ministering to in this locality, doctor?'

'You pin this on Father Crosby and it's you who will have to examine your consciences. You'll be giving whoever actually did this free rein to do it again. When we spoke on Tuesday you had a list. What has become of that?'

'Peter McLaughlin has a rock-solid alibi: us. Francie Quinn can account for his whereabouts. Dick Bruton is a bit shaky, but frankly if he had done it we would have found out already by the trail of watery, yellow shite he'd have left leading all the way back to him. Jack O'Riordain was teaching school and seems to have been the first to realise that Liam was missing when he took the roll. You don't have a dick. So that leaves Crosby. And he already admitted to us that he was on the Castlebar road Monday morning, close to where Liam's body was put in the water.'

'Jesus, I wasted that Sherlock Holmes on you. Textbooks in deductive and abductive reasoning and the best you boys can come up with is, "Here's someone we don't understand: let's lynch him for it." I presume this is why the Irish people in our wisdom came up with the term "gobshite": to more fully describe eejits such as yourselves.'

We said nothing.

'You boys are missing something,' Dr Hennessy continued. 'It simply can't be Martin, and if you knew the man you would not be buying into this pile of shite. Now, as you are well aware, I have plenty of patients to be seeing, so I'll bid you both on your way.'

'We have a few more questions, Doctor,' said Eamon.

'Well, I have no more answers for you. So, if I haven't been clear let me repeat myself: fuck off out of my surgery.'

At that she stood up, walked to the door and opened it. We stood up and followed her to the door. It was the fiercest tongue lashing that I had received from a woman in about fifteen years, since the last time my ma had scalped my arse.

'Thanks for your time, Doctor,' I managed to croak as I left. She said nothing and slammed the door behind us. The frosted glass rattled in its frame so violently that, for a moment, I thought it might shatter.

XX

We trudged down the street wheeling our bikes to McLaughlin's office. He was sequestered away, according to Bronagh, meeting with a client but should be finished in half an hour or so. We filled the time by making tea.

It wasn't the first time that we had made Bronagh a cup of tea, but from her reaction you would think it was. She gave us a beaming smile before we headed back into the kitchen, which, for want of any other sort of accommodation, we had made into our own. I suppose tea-making generally being seen as part of her job description she considered it an enormous treat when someone bothered their arse to fetch her one instead.

'Bronagh has got great dimples when she smiles, don't you think?' I said to Eamon as we sat down. Uncharacteristically he did not take the bait, he just grunted an affirmative.

'Chess?' I asked.

This time he grunted a negative and so I pulled a Holmes and Watson volume out of my satchel and started to read as Eamon sipped his tea and looked out the window.

After a while we heard footsteps on the stairs and hearty farewells as McLaughlin saw his client out of the office. As the door closed we heard his footsteps approach the kitchen.

'I understand you boys wanted to see me?'

'We do, but we'd have come to your office.'

'Not a bother, fellas. Sure I've been sitting on my arse for the past two hours and it's good to get up and move around.'

'Can I make you a cup of tea?' I asked as he sat down.

'That would be great, Mick. Thanks.'

I put the kettle back on so as to be able to make a fresh pot. 'So,' said McLaughlin, 'what's the craic?'

'It's about Liam Finnegan.'

'Go on.'

'On Tuesday we had a walk along the river and found where we believe young Liam went into the water.'

'What made you think that?'

'We found what we believe was the remains of the sandwich his mother had made him for breakfast after Mass alongside tyre tracks. We concluded from this that whoever put him in the water had driven him there in a car. There are six people in town who own cars. Dr Hennessy, Francie Quinn, Dick Bruton, Jack O'Riordain, Father Crosby and yourself.' Eamon paused.

McLaughlin barely reacted to that. 'Go on,' he repeated.

'We questioned Dick Bruton. He was in the vicinity of where Liam was put in the water in the timeframe in which Liam was put in the water. But it's difficult seeing Bruton doing it and, apart from that, no indication that Liam was anywhere near him on Monday. Francie Quinn gives a reasonable account of his whereabouts in the timeframe in question and says his wife can vouch for him. Jack O'Riordain we have not spoken to yet, but he would've been teaching school. You don't appear to have had the opportunity.'

'Why not?'

'You were in the office when Bronagh got here at nine. Liam seems to have been lifted between the end of eight o'clock Mass and nine, when he should have been at school.'

'I could have taken him straight from Mass, could I not?'

That took us by surprise. 'What?' I asked.

'I was at eight o'clock Mass. I usually go and come here straight after.' Myself and Eamon looked at each other. 'Jaysus, boys, for budding detectives you are lacking in curiosity in some key departments. What did ye think? That my entire life is built around conveyancing and petty claims?'

'I suppose with that and the parish court, I did, aye,' I said, and I set down the cup of tea on the kitchen table beside him.

McLaughlin let out a bit of a chuckle and added some milk from a jug on the table. Looking back I imagine he must have wondered at the discrepancy between who he had been and who he had become. He once had been young, fallen in love, and raised a son. Now for the most part he just mostly worked. Or perhaps he was wondering at the difference between how he thought of himself and how he was seen by others. He was, after all, not just a country solicitor but a revolutionary, even if not a dashing flying column commander.

'What about the rest?' he asked.

'Dr Hennessy is not a suspect for obvious reasons.'

'Why obvious?'

'She is a woman.'

'You think a woman couldn't hurt a child?'

'No. I'm quite sure a woman could be as violent and murderous as any man, save in one respect.'

'What is that?'

'Liam was anally raped.'

For a moment there was silence. Eamon had not been that forensic about the nature of Liam's sexual assault up to this point and I found the words jarring. I can only imagine the impact that they were having on McLaughlin.

After a moment he said two words. 'Jesus wept.'

'He did,' said Eamon.

'You did not mention this before.'

'I did not.'

'Why not?'

'Army habit, I'm afraid, Peter: only tell your officers the bare minimum you have to.'

I saw a semblance of anger passing across Peter's face.

'I'm sorry, Peter,' said Eamon before Peter could say anything. He reached into his satchel which was at his feet and withdrew the folder that Dr Hennessy had given us.

'This is the report of the post-mortem report that Dr Hennessy conducted.' Peter opened it and spent a few minutes scanning the pages in silence. Then he reached into his jacket pocket and pulled out a packet of cigarettes and a box of matches. He did not offer any around but lit one without taking his eyes from the report pages. After a while he looked up from the report but said nothing until he had finished his cigarette which he then ground out in the ashtray on the kitchen table.

'Whenever I was a youngster I thought criminal law would be more interesting than any other sort. This sort of sick shite reminds me why I turned my back on it.'

'I heard tell you'd been involved in a murder case once,' I said.

'I was,' said Peter. 'Some poor eejit put a pitchfork into the husband of a woman he'd been carrying on with. Him and the woman both went to the gallows. Not a brain cell between the two of them, God love them. Planned it together and then tried to pass it off as self-defence. They neither went to the bother of getting their stories straight, nor of considering the rather elementary possibility of witnesses.'

'Who saw them?'

'The man's children. Woken up in the middle of the night by the ructions and saw the whole barbarous thing.'

'Jesus,' I said. 'Imagine having to carry that about with you all the rest of your life: seeing your father murdered and then helping send your mother to the gallows.'

'Indeed,' said Peter. 'But at least they had their lives left to them. Which is not the case here. Likewise we seem to be short of witnesses. So what else do you know?'

'Dr Hennessy also assures us she did not lend her car to anyone. Which leaves us with Father Crosby.'

'What about him?'

'Liam was serving his Mass at eight o'clock.'

'I know,' said McLaughlin.

'So far as we can ascertain he was the last person to see Liam alive. His story is problematic, indicating a particular and unusual affection for Liam. He has a car and he admits to being on the road between here and Castlebar and so would have had ample opportunity to put Liam in the water. So, from where I'm looking, he had motive, means and opportunity.'

'Some physical evidence would be helpful too. Or a confession?'

'We have neither of those, I'm afraid,' said Eamon. 'Crosby's saying nothing, but I think something's bothering him. And I've heard enough sordid stories about the way priests carry on to be concerned.'

'Where did you hear them stories, Eamon? From some fire-and-brimstone preacher from up north? No offence, Mick.'

'None taken,' I said.

'From my wife. She was a nurse and she treated some of the girls who found themselves the playthings of the clergy.'

'Well, I don't mean to cast aspersions on your late wife, Eamon. But whatever happened in Paris ten years ago hardly has any evidentiary value in what we are dealing with now.'

Peter took a sip of the tea I had made for him and was quiet for a while. Then he said, 'This is good work so far, lads. But we will need a bit more than that if we are going to haul him up in front of the circuit court on charges of rape and murder.'

'With respect, Peter, are you perhaps letting your commitment to the Church get in the way of your objectivity?'

I expected Peter to bridle at that but he was calmness itself. 'On the contrary, Eamon, I think it is you who may be letting your antipathy to the clergy get in the way of your objectivity in this instance. Priest or not, I never did have much time for that Crosby fella. But that's rather beside the point. We simply don't have enough to take this to the circuit court yet. Ideally, we should have physical evidence. But you also need to have a closer look at Bruton. See if you can find anything that will rule him in or rule him out.'

Then he reached his hand in his trouser pocket and pulled out a car key. 'I presume you can drive, Eamon?'

'I can,' said Eamon. 'The British Army was good for a few things.'

'Grand so. Take my car up to the church and see how long it takes you to drive from there to where you think Liam was put in the water. See whether that expands or contracts your suspicions about me.'

'We don't actually think you did this, Peter,' I said.

'No matter,' said Peter. 'If we want to present this to a court of law, we must be thorough. And whether I am under any real suspicion or otherwise, it will be useful to see just how long that little excursion takes.'

'Okay,' I said.

'And you still haven't spoken to Jack O'Riordain yet.'

'Aye,' said Eamon. 'About that. Francie Quinn mentioned that he met Jack on the road on Monday, about lunchtime. When we asked him what it was about he told us to mind our own business. Except he was less polite about it than that.'

'So?' asked McLaughlin.

'Well, Francie was suspicious that you had not briefed him on our enquiries. And my instinct would suggest that Francie is providing concrete military or logistical support to the forces of the Republic, which is a new departure for Francie, if I'm not mistaken. But if Jack gets wind from Francie that we have been prying into such confidential matters he may take some umbrage. The sort of umbrage that could get us plugged in the nut if we are not too careful.'

'I wouldn't worry about that,' said McLaughlin. 'I'll speak to Francie and tell him you are conducting a legitimate enquiry under the authority of the Courts of the Irish Republic.'

'That's as may be,' said Eamon, 'but those peelers at the barracks had also made some legitimate enquiries about protections afforded them under the laws of war, which, frankly, Jack wasn't too arsed about at the time.'

'Hmm,' said McLaughlin. 'Look, Eamon. I know you and Jack have had your differences, but I have always found him to be a fair man. I know, as you heard yourself, he regrets profoundly what happened at the barracks. But you know yourself the sort of excesses that can happen in battle.'

'The battle was over when he shot them.'

'Come on, Eamon,' said McLaughlin. 'You heard what he said about that yourself at Liam's funeral. We are in a war. We cannot have everything as we would like it. Currently the Dáil courts have no authority over military matters. Which means that I have no authority over Jack. So in these circumstances we have to cooperate as Irishmen with common purpose. Things will be easier when we are at peace, when the dogs of war are leashed again.'

'So we'll go and have a word with Jack about what he was doing tearing about the countryside on Monday on what was plainly military business, and hope for the best.'

'You speak to Jack, just as you have spoken to me, to eliminate him from our enquiries, as you are legally empowered to do by Dáil Éireann through the court system that our democratically elected parliament has established. I will speak to Jack in my capacity as chair of the parish court and explain what ye are up to and request his patriotic cooperation.'

Eamon didn't look happy. And frankly, as the conversation had progressed I had become increasingly unsettled.

'We all have our duties here, Eamon,' McLaughlin said.

'Aye, I suppose,' said Eamon, but he didn't look any happier.

'Have a fag,' said McLaughlin and he tossed his packet to Eamon. Eamon caught them and extracted one and stuck it between his lips. McLaughlin retrieved the packet from Eamon, drew out another cigarette for himself and then lit them both up. This time he seemed to remember that I did not smoke.

'Boys, we are trying to make a new nation here. If it was easy, they would not write history books about it. But if we succeed we will have something we have not had in nine hundred years. Our own country. Now, I know you fellas think you got stuck with the shitty end of the stick when you were assigned to me to help me manage the courts and enforce the rulings of petty sessions. But what we are doing here is, I believe, at least as important as what the local brigades and flying columns are doing, reducing the police barracks and pinning the Crown forces down into the big towns. It may be difficult to see right now, but what we are doing is vital to creating an actual Republic, not just the imaginary one that Pearse and his fellow nutcases were prattling on about. Because it's not killing and "blood sacrifice" that makes a nation. It's taking care of each other and protecting the weak that does that. What we are doing here can help show the world that we can run our own affairs, that due process and the rule of law will be fundamental to who we are and who we wish to become. And that no one is above the law.'

'Except when they are shooting unarmed peelers after they have surrendered,' said Eamon.

'We can only do our best with the resources that we have, Eamon. Now if you'll forgive me, I've a bit more conveyancing and petty claims to be getting on with.' He winked at me. 'But I'll take this with me,' he said lifting Dr Hennessy's medical report from the kitchen table. 'I want to read it again later.'

He stood up. 'That was a grand cup of tea, Mick. Thanks very much. And let me know how ye get on with Jack. Just try not to antagonise him when you see him, will you? I'll speak to Francie and Jack tonight or tomorrow. Assure them that you are conducting enquiries under my instructions and that they have nothing to worry about from a military perspective.' He left the kitchen and went back up the stairs to his office.

'Fuck,' I said.

'Succinctly put,' said Eamon.

XXI

Over the next hour or so we discovered two things. First that Eamon had been somewhat economical with the truth when he said he could drive. The car jumped about like a violent jack rabbit as he tried to refamiliarise himself with clutch control. Second that it took just over seven minutes to get from the church to the spot where we thought Liam's body had been put in the water.

We ran back and forth from church to the dumping point twice to make sure we had the timing right. On neither trip did we see another soul either turning off the road, nor once we had turned off it.

As we had the car we decided we'd see if we could catch O'Riordain for the conversation that neither of us wanted to have with him. Given the hour, we went first to his house.

According to Eamon, O'Riordain was an only child who was now the sole resident of the house he had inherited when his mother died shortly before the outbreak of the war. His father, Eamon said, had been a violent drunk who had died years before when he had fallen in the river one winter's night when, much the worse for wear, he had paused to have a piss in it on the way home from Toner's.

'You said you were at school with him,' I said to Eamon.

'He was a year or so ahead of me at school. A cunt then too, but a bright cunt. Got him a scholarship to teacher training college.'

'How long has he been headmaster here?'

'Since the end of 1913. He'd been teaching a couple of

years in Dublin, I think, but decided to come home when the position became vacant here.'

'And that was when he joined the Volunteers too?'

'Aye. He had been in one of the Dublin units from the start but transferred to our lot when he moved back.'

'But he didn't follow Redmond into the civilising ranks of the British Army.'

'No. Maybe if I had managed to get one of those scholarships myself I would have read sufficient to have the gumption not to be eejit enough to believe all that "rights of small nations" guff they were spouting back then in order to get us join up.'

'Ah,' I said, 'but look at the man it made you.'

'You know, Mick,' Eamon said, 'I think I would still prefer to be the man I once was.'

O'Riordain was absent from home when we got there, so without much expectation that we would find him, we went back up to the school to see if he was there. He wasn't. I don't know how Eamon felt, but I was profoundly relieved that the confrontation had been averted, if only temporarily.

We drove back to McLaughlin's and left the keys with Bronagh, who was getting ready to go home. She gave us one of her smiles as we left.

We walked back up the street towards Toner's. As we drew near I had a reluctant thought: 'Shouldn't we try to have a word with Dick?'

'I was afraid you were going to say that, Mick,' and without another word we crossed the street and entered Bruton's general store.

Bruton blanched as we entered. 'Take it easy, Dick,' said Eamon, 'we just need a word.'

'What is it, boys?' asked Bruton.

'In private if you could be so kind.'

'We can go out the back to my office,' he said with a hint of trepidation in his voice. Then, '*Roisin!*' he shouted across the shop. Roisin, a brown-eyed young woman with her black hair tied back, appeared from the storeroom at the back of the shop. I recognised her as the girl who had been helping with tea and sandwiches at Liam's wake.

'What is it?' she asked.

'Keep an eye on the place while I go and have a word with these gentlemen.'

Bruton led us out the back of the shop and down a short corridor into a small office with a desk and two chairs. 'Shall I get another chair?' Bruton asked.

'Not at all,' I said. 'I'm happy to stand.'

Bruton sat down beside his desk. Sweat was already beading on his forehead and upper lip. Eamon took the other chair. I closed the office door and stood with my back against it.

'So what can I help you with, boys? Is it to do with your logistics?'

I could not help feeling intensely sorry for Bruton at this point. He was clearly terrified and hoping that being helpful would improve matters for him. In retrospect, my towering over him and barring the door to the exit can't have made things easier. But as usual I said nothing and allowed Eamon to do the running.

'Not this time, Dick,' said Eamon.

'So what can I help you with?' asked Bruton.

'Did you see Liam Finnegan on Monday morning?'

'No. Like I told you already I went off early to Castlebar.'

'Refresh my memory please, Dick. What time did you say you went off?'

'About nine.'

'Can anybody verify your whereabouts up to your departure for Castlebar?'

'I was in the house with the wife, so she could.'

'So if we ask your wife now were you in the house up until nine o'clock and your departure for Castlebar, she would confirm that?'

'She would… Except she's gone over to her sister's for the evening and won't be back until late. What's this about, boys?'

Eamon looked at me and raised his eyebrows as if asking the question, 'Do you buy this?'

I nodded. I had thought this crime did not fit Bruton from the last time we spoke to him. I would have happily put money on his wife confirming his alibi.

'Okay, Dick,' said Eamon. 'Thanks for your time. But I must ask you not to repeat this conversation or any elements of it to anyone else, not even your wife.'

'Why?' asked Bruton. 'What is this about?'

'Can't tell you that,' said Eamon. 'And remember, you are still on thin ice with us, Dick. So best be a good boy.'

Eamon stood and I opened the office door. He walked past me back into the body of the shop. I was about to follow him but thought 'I can't just leave it like that', so I turned back to face him. 'Thanks, Dick,' I said. 'And take it easy. You've been a great help. In time you will understand what a service to the Republic you have done today.' Then I followed Eamon into the shop, and out onto the street.

XXII

'So what, in the name of fuck, was all that shite about "service to the Republic"?' asked Eamon.

We were sitting in the back of Toner's in the snug.

'I was feeling sorry for the man. I thought the least we could do is throw the poor fucker some sort of a bone.'

Eamon let out a sigh. 'You're a kind-hearted fellow, Mick,' he said. 'That's the sort of thing can get you plugged very easy if you are not careful.'

'How in the name of God can kindness get someone killed?'

'There was a fellow, Vic Brotherton, an English fellow I met once during the war. He tried to save my life. Crawled out to me in broad daylight when he had seen me hit in no man's land. I'm not going to lie to you. It hurt like a bastard and I was bawling like a little girl. It was probably that that turned Brotherton to such heroic decency. "Don't worry, chum, I'll get you," he kept saying as he came towards me. Got him a mention in dispatches and a bullet through his ear for his troubles.'

'Fuck,' I said. 'Poor bastard. So how come you are not actually dead, then?'

'Two stretcher-bearers came out after dark, brought me in.'

'You didn't bleed to death when you were waiting?'

'I had the presence of mind to stuff my wound with scraps of Vic's uniform while I was waiting.'

'So he saved your life in the end?'

'At the cost of his own.'

'So the moral of the story is: if you are going to be kind, be careful.'

'No, the moral of the story is kindness is for peacetime. When you are in the middle of a war you do your job. Let other people do their job and hope it all turns out right. It's not your job or my job to soft-soap Bruton. He has a wife for that. It's our job to find out who killed Liam, and hopefully put a stop to the fucker hurting any more kids ever again.'

I said nothing but I still thought in some particular way, which I could not quite put my finger on, that he was wrong. In the absence of anything witty or intelligent to say I drained my pint. 'I think it's your round so,' I said.

'Jesus, you're drinking very fast. I'm not finished yet.'

'But I am. Jesus, Eamon, how long were you out of Ireland that the most cherished traditions of this proud land of ours have come to mean so little to you, that you can contemplate with such equanimity a man at your table with an empty glass? Do you want your name cursed for seven generations at every hearth and fireside from West Connaught to South Ulster?'

Eamon laughed at that and got to his feet. He returned after a few minutes with the beer. We took a drink of our pints and looked at each other.

'You know,' said Eamon, 'the Dutch once invented a resealable beer bottle?'

'Jesus,' I said. 'What sort of barbaric nation does that sorta thing?'

'Fucked if I know,' said Eamon. 'But that's a fact.'

'Where did you hear tell of it?'

'A Belgian fella told me during the war. So it must be true. He also told me that the Dutch subsist almost entirely on cheese so that may have induced some sort of obscure dementia that makes them think that beer should sometimes be consumed in measures smaller than a pint. Say what you like about the English but they've never inflicted that sort of obscenity on humanity.'

'No, just colonialism, the slave trade, the odd famine, and worst of all, that holier than thou attitude that still seems to pervade their every utterance on the moral failings of others.'

'Ach, look at it from their perspective, Mick. Many of them have not the least clue about their own history towards other peoples. And them that do, well, human beings seem to have a need to tell themselves that even when they do the most grotesque things, probably especially when they do the most grotesque things, that they are still good people. The amount of shite that the British have done over the centuries, they have had to convince themselves they are the best people the world has ever seen.'

I thought about that for a moment. 'Like Agamemnon,' I said.

'Enlighten me there, Mick.'

'Before they set sail for Troy to recapture Helen, the Greek fleet was threatened with destruction by a storm sent by the goddess Artemis. The soothsayers examined the entrails and advised Agamemnon that if he wished to placate the goddess then he must pay tribute to her by sacrificing his own daughter. So he did just that. Artemis was placated and off they went to reclaim Helen and raze Troy to the ground.'

'That "ends justifies the means" shite?'

'No, it was worse than that. As he had the child trussed up and slaughtered like a goat, Agamemnon paraded himself before the army as if he were a moral paragon and his butchery of his own daughter was a virtuous thing.'

'Murder as a higher form of morality, then?'

'Aye, that sort of thing.'

'Aye, the English are past masters at that oul shite too. Their entire colonial project based on it, in fact. Maybe our problem, Mick, is that we don't pay enough attention to classical education in this country. We have no hope of a global empire until we can murder the defenceless like that and then convince ourselves and everyone else that we are morally good because we have done so.'

'Oh, I don't know,' I said. 'Jack seems to be doing well in that regard.'

'Perhaps he is destined for greatness, then?'

'Just like the English.'

'Aye, just like the English. True imperial greatness insists that we show more sympathy for those that do the crucifying rather than them that are crucified.'

'Lucky for them they murdered all those poor people in Amritsar last year then.'

'Exactly. If they hadn't done that they might have begun to realise that they are ordinary human beings like the rest of us, instead of God's latest Chosen People, appointed by Jehovah himself to rule the waves and be his sword to the unworthy.'

'God help them if the boot is ever on the other foot.'

'Jaysus, can you imagine it! The shock they would have when they discover Indians remember all the shite they have forgotten. The English will be going on like, "But we built you your railways. Why are you being so mean to us now?" And the Indians will be remembering that long catalogue of imperial atrocities that God's finally granted them a moment of reckoning for. If what goes around really does come around the English have a massive and bloody pile of shite to look forward to.'

'I suppose Shakespeare redeems them a bit.'

'If he was English.'

'You think he wasn't?'

'Who else but a Paddy is going to have a Danish prince, who has just seen the ghost of his da, praying to St Patrick as he contemplates murdering his uncle?'

'I didn't know that we had a reputation for wanting to regularly murder uncles?'

'Maybe that's just Sligo men. I mean, you complain about me being slow to buy a pint. Those boys have the shortest fingers and the longest pockets on the entire island of Ireland. They're the sort of fellas you really should never trust your ageing relatives to the care of. They'd die of thirst before Hamlet had finished his soliloquy.'

'Do you have a specific prejudice against every county in Ireland, Eamon?'

'Just the ones that are prejudiced against me.'

'And Sligo men have a particular prejudice against you?'

'They seem to. Well, Mayo men in general, I think. Before I got my own stripes I suffered under the attention of a particularly obnoxious corporal, from Dundalk of all places he was, who gave me a dog's time on account, he said, of me coming from Mayo.'

'So now you have a specific prejudice against Louth too?'

'Actually, I'm giving Louth the benefit of the doubt on this one. This fellow told me he picked up his prejudice when he was working in Sligo. So this one is still on them.'

'That's a bit of a relief. I always had a soft spot for the Dundalk girls. They had a certain air of exoticism about them, compared to them from where I was from.'

'The daughters of Cuchulainn, sort of thing?'

'Never thought of it that way. 'Tis the sort of thing Yeats would say though.'

Eamon snorted. 'Come to think of it, it is.'

'Have you read much of him?'

'Always reading a bit of Yeats. It took me a while to get to like him, but he really is something extraordinary.'

'Doesn't he buy Sligo a little of your indulgence then?'

'Sure, Yeats is just a Dub who went on his summer holidays there. I mean you're hardly a Mayo man just because you've spent a few weeks here. And I've hardly become French despite spending the best part of four years there.'

'He can write though.'

'Lord Jesus, he can. Greatest poet since Shakespeare. You see? Yet more evidence for my theory about Willie's true Celtic origins. That scale of genius can only really be Irish!'

'Aye, you make a strong point, Eamon, there's no doubt about that. But I have difficulty seeing the serried ranks of British academia ever agreeing with you.'

'Ah sure, fuck them,' he said with a smile and raised his glass to me. I raised mine back and clinked his.

'To Irish genius then,' I said.

'Slainte,' said Eamon, and we both took another slug on our pints.

'So are we two geniuses any closer to finding out who killed Liam?' Eamon asked as we set down our pints.

'Well, I think we can rule Bruton out now.'

'Agreed. And Peter.'

'So we are left with Crosby and O'Riordain.'

'Aye. If we can believe Jack had the time to fuck him, murder him and take the fifteen minutes there and back to dump him in the river before taking class register at nine o'clock on Monday.'

'So that leaves us with your little fixation on Crosby. What if Dr Hennessy is right and if we pin it on him whoever is doing this will be left free to carry on?'

'So who amongst our candidates do you feel has a better claim on that elusive formula of motive, means and opportunity? Particularly opportunity?'

'I don't know. But much as I hate to admit it, Peter is right. We have to speak to Jack.'

'School starts at nine o'clock. Liam left the church at eight-thirty. Not much opportunity.'

'When I was at primary school the headmaster used to come in late from time to time. Nobody would say anything to him. He was the headmaster. And I imagine with battalion business Jack has more excuse than most to arrive late from time to time.'

'Hmm.'

'Or perhaps he lent his car to some passing Dub who was feeling a bit lonely and decided to create a bit of a home away from home with young Liam.'

'You think all Dubs fuck their young?'

'I have been attentive to your wise words since I got here, Eamon.'

'It's possible, I suppose, that there was someone else involved other than our local car owners. There is always those occasional visits from headquarters to bring those depraved Pale-dwellers into our midst.'

'Have there been any such visits of late?'

'Fucked if I know,' said Eamon. 'As our encounter with Francie Quinn so starkly demonstrated, we are not generally privy to information on military developments. But I'm still inclined to think it must have been someone who knew Liam already. There is a certain air of calculation to what happened to him. I don't think that's something that a passing stranger could have achieved.'

'So what next?' I asked.

'Let's try and have another word with Jack. Tomorrow morning. Before school.'

'Because those early morning interviews always go so well?'

'On the bright side, Jack is teetotal. So we won't be poking a bear with a sore head this time.'

'No,' I said. 'Just, according to you, a cunt with a grudge and thirty armed men who he has already schooled in the art of murder.'

FRIDAY

XXIII

WE RENDEZVOUSED AT McLaughlin's office at half past seven. I don't remember ever having been so nervous. I'd already spent a good portion of the morning in the outhouse, shitting out a considerable portion of my guts.

Eamon seemed all composure. But it was just façade as he said, 'I have something for you.' He reached into his satchel and withdrew a short-barrelled Webley revolver. 'You ever use one of these?'

'No,' I said.

'Well, it's not particularly difficult. Six chambers, but it is advisable to carry only five rounds and keep the hammer on the empty chamber to prevent the sort of little accidents that might blow your dick off. This one is already loaded. When you pull back the hammer to cock it the magazine will rotate and bring a round into position.' He cocked the revolver to show me what he meant.

'See?' he asked.

'Aye.'

Eamon made the weapon safe again.

'Now,' he continued, 'if you do have to shoot it, do not aim. Hold it with two hands, none of that one-handed cowboy shite you might have seen at the pictures' – he demonstrated the proper grip – 'and point it at the middle of what you want to hit. Two shots, if you can manage to get them off, is usually enough.'

I began to reach out, but then hesitated. 'Shouldn't you keep it?' I asked.

'I have another,' he said and lifted his jacket to show the butt of another revolver tucked into his belt at the small of his back. 'I acquired this one in the army. Yours, I picked up from the police barracks when our comrades were busy shooting the survivors.'

He reached in his pocket and withdrew a handful of bullets. 'Here's ten extra rounds, just in case.' I took them from him and put them in my left-hand jacket pocket, and then copied Eamon by lodging the revolver in my belt at the small of my back.

'Okay so,' said Eamon, 'no putting this off, I suppose.'

We mounted up and cycled over to Jack O'Riordain's house. It was a long, low white-washed cottage with a black slate roof. There was a light on in the kitchen as we approached. The kitchen hearth and tea offered no prospect of comfort on this miserable November morning. Instead it filled me with trepidation: there would be no avoiding the confrontation this time.

We leaned our bicycles against the gable wall of O'Riordain's house, out of the wind, and rapped the door. We immediately heard footsteps approaching from the kitchen and then his voice.

'Who is it?' he shouted through the door.

'Eamon, and Mick McAlinden. Mr McLaughlin asked us to speak to you on a court-related matter.'

'Just yourselves?' shouted O'Riordain.

''Tis.'

We heard the door being unbolted and then it swung open. O'Riordain stood there in shirt and trousers, his boots on and, ready for anything, a Mauser automatic pistol loosely held by his side.

'Miserable morning, fellows,' he said. 'Well, come in out of that. All the heat is getting out.'

We stepped over the threshold and he motioned us down his hallway into the kitchen. If truth be told there was not much heat to be letting out into the winter air. The place was cold and dark, until we got into the kitchen, which was an oasis of warmth.

'Have a seat so,' he said. He lifted something from a sideboard which I realised was the Mauser's wooden holster. I knew the holster doubled as a detachable stock when the user needed to take more careful aim. O'Riordain affixed the stock to the pistol now and then set the assembled weapon back on the sideboard before turning to us. 'Do ye want a cup of tea?'

It was an altogether warmer reception than I thought we had any right to expect after the altercation outside Liam's funeral.

'Aye, that would be great so,' said Eamon.

O'Riordain lifted two blue willow-patterned cups down from a shelf and set them before us. 'There you go: the good china for the visitors, just like my mother always told me.' Then he turned to the cooking range and lifted the teapot from it and poured us both our tea. The milk and sugar were already on the table so we doctored it according to our tastes as O'Riordain topped up his own mug of tea. He sat down on another kitchen chair beside the sideboard and the Mauser. 'So what's the craic?' he asked.

Eamon started. 'Did you see Mr McLaughlin yesterday at all?'

'No.'

'Well, he had wanted to brief you personally before we met you. He has asked us to make a few enquiries on behalf of the parish court about the death of Liam Finnegan.'

'Why's that? I thought it was just a tragic accident.'

'Well, we had hoped that we might be able to prevent some future such tragic accidents.'

'Jaysus,' said O'Riordain. 'You can prevent such tragic accidents in future by putting the fear of God into children about mitching off school and messing around close to dangerous water. For fuck sake! Whenever I assigned you boys to the Irish Republican Police I was under the impression that there was vital war work to be done. Sounds to me like McLaughlin has you boys on a wild goose chase. Perhaps I should have you reassigned back to the battalion? Or perhaps duties in the flying column would be more appealing? Certainly more suited to a man with your military experience, Eamon. I can recommend you both to brigade for that.'

'I thought you said I was no more use as a fighting man,' said Eamon.

'Indeed, I did,' said O'Riordain, 'and I'm sorry for that. I think I spoke too harshly. Not everyone has the capacity to make the hard decisions of leadership, but that does not mean his contribution cannot be important. And after the good reports that Peter has been giving of ye, I thought that perhaps I was being too short-sighted about you. And the flying columns can use men with experience for the job they have to do.'

The thought went through my mind: 'Then the devil led Him up to a high place and showed Him in an instant all the kingdoms of the world.'

'Well, I wouldn't say no to a flying column assignment,' said Eamon. 'But in the meantime we do need to clear up this matter for Peter.'

'So what do you want to know?'

'About what time did you get to school at on Monday morning?'

'The normal time. Nine-ish.'

'Nothing unusual that morning to delay you?'

'I had a few battalion matters to deal with first thing but nothing too out of the ordinary.'

'Anybody able to confirm that?'

''Twas mostly paperwork, reports for HQ and the like. Easier to work on that sort of thing when I'm on my own.'

'Francie Quinn said he saw you on the road about lunchtime.'

'Indeed.'

'Can you tell us what that was about?'

'No.'

'Military matters?'

'Indeed. I will confirm that much.'

'Can you tell us if you had left school specifically to see Quinn?'

'I had. He wasn't about the house when I called so I was heading back to school when I bumped into him on the road.'

'Have you lent your car to anyone recently?'

'Hold on there, fellows. You said you wanted to ask me about Liam's death. I cannot see what any of this has to do with that.'

'Just a few anomalies relating to Liam's death.'

'A youngster drowns in a tragic accident and you boys use that as an excuse to start prying into military matters that frankly don't concern you? Now, from where I'm sitting, this does begin to look suspicious.' O'Riordain's manner remained affable, but that did not disguise his menace one single iota.

'As I said, we are simply following Mr McLaughlin's instructions.'

'Well, I think before I answer another single question off you boys I will need to speak to Peter. You have got to see it from my point of view,' said O'Riordain. 'You two show up, an ex-British Army non-commissioned officer, and a man from God knows where in the Black North, and you start prying. That to me smacks of intelligence gathering. And I'm damned if I am going to allow informers to destroy this rebellion in the way that they have destroyed every other in Irish history.'

'We are not informers,' I said. 'We are sworn officers of the Irish Republican Police and we are following our own orders to enquire into the unusual circumstances surrounding the death of Liam Finnegan.'

'And yet you have asked me fuck all about that, but instead are enquiring into matters that are of a confidential military nature in this parish.'

I was about to say straight out that Liam had been murdered by someone with a car. But Eamon got in first.

'I do see your point, Commandant. We are not informers, as Mick has so forcefully put it, but you have your own responsibilities to the Republic, as do we. So we will cease our conversation here until Mr McLaughlin has had the opportunity to speak to you and explain the situation in more depth.'

'Okay so. But if I do not hear from him today, I will really be getting suspicious.'

'That is clear, Commandant.'

We pushed our chairs back as we stood up. 'Thanks for your time.'

'After you, gentlemen,' said O'Riordain. I looked at the distance between Jack and the Mauser before I turned. For a moment I wondered if he was going to act on his suspicion and put a couple of bullets in our backs as we walked down the hallway. I looked at Eamon seeking some reassurance, but his face was drawn and pale. 'Go on, Mick,' he said and I walked towards the door, conscious at every step of the thump of O'Riordain's boots behind me.

The morning was beginning to break as we got to the door, but with it, it was bringing miserable weather, with the rain beginning to splatter off a chilling east wind.

'The three coldest things in the world,' said O'Riordain from the door. 'An east wind, a dog's nose, and a woman's heart.' He laughed mirthlessly. 'I'd better hear from Peter by the end of the day, boys,' and closed the door behind us.

'Cunt,' said Eamon.

XXIV

We arrived back at McLaughlin's office just as he himself was driving up, Mass, I presumed, having finished a few minutes earlier.

'How's it going boys?' he asked.

'It's been better,' said Eamon.

'Well, let's get out of this wind and you can tell me about it.'

He unlocked the door and we followed him into the kitchen, where he got the kettle on.

'So,' he said. 'What's the craic?'

'We've just come from O'Riordain's.'

'How did that go?'

'Not the best. He told us he had got to the school at nine-ish. He'd been at home alone up to that. He confirmed that he has been engaged with Quinn in some military-related project. And he told us he regarded our questioning as suspicious and that unless you confirmed to him today that we were on official business, he would likely have us shot as informers.'

'Jaysus, Eamon! I told you not to antagonise him!'

'Eamon did not antagonise him,' I said. 'He was courtesy itself from start to finish. O'Riordain was also perfectly pleasant, even giving us tea, right up to the point that he started threatening to have us plugged!'

'Hmm,' said Peter. 'Well, I imagine he has a right to be a bit jumpy. The weather is probably the only thing keeping the Black and Tans at bay at the moment. Once it improves there'll be a counter-offensive and whatever chances the IRA will have against them are going to be dependent on them keeping a tight ship and strong discipline.'

'I didn't say it wasn't understandable. Just, and I would like to reiterate this matter for the nth time, just that we would rather see out the year not being consigned to some bog hole with bullets in our brains.'

'Look,' said McLaughlin. 'I've a couple of meetings this morning, but I'll go up to the school before lunchtime and speak to him. You didn't find out if he had lent his car to anyone, did you?'

'No. That was the point he shut down the conversation.'

'Okay. I'll ask him about that too. Anything else we want to know?'

'Well, we'd like to know definitively whether or not he fucked and strangled Liam. And, if he didn't, does he know, by any chance, who did.'

Peter snorted. 'He may not volunteer sufficient verifiable information for us on that particular matter, Eamon. But I'll see what I can do.'

'Anything you want us to do in the meantime, Peter?'

'Tell you what, boys, take it a bit easy today. Even in the service of the Republic I would say one death threat is enough for any day.'

XXV

After Peter had gone off to his office, Eamon suggested we go over to his home for breakfast. It was the first time he'd invited me to his. He lived with his widowed mother, his older brother, and his new sister-in-law on the edge of town. His brother, Brendan, had inherited the family forge, but Eamon helped out a bit from time to time. It was basic agricultural work for the most part, shoeing horses, sharpening scythes and the like. But Brendan also did some bicycle repairs and Eamon did a bit of tinkering with the occasional engine, having picked up some of the rudiments of repairs in the British Army.

Brendan also had a bit of a sideline in the manufacture of bombs and land mines for the IRA, but he tended to conduct this business away from the forge in an outhouse at the end of a small paddock the family owned.

Brendan was working in the forge when we arrived. He hailed us from across the top of his anvil as we passed. I had met him down in Toner's once before and he seemed like a decent man, warm and open, like an older version of Eamon but without the world weariness or cynicism, without the war. Brendan's presence in Toner's was a rare one because, as Eamon put it, he preferred to spend his evenings 'fucking the wife'. Once I saw the modest-sized home they shared I presumed that this was maybe why, conversely, Eamon liked to spend so much time down the pub.

Eamon's mother was the only one about the place when we arrived. His sister-in-law, Fiona, was off to Bruton's shopping.

Mrs Gleason welcomed me like the Prodigal returned. 'I've heard a lot about you, Mick. How are you finding it in the wilds of the west? A bit different from what you are used to, I suppose?'

'Ach, it's not so different,' I said. 'Poor Catholic farmers have it the same over most of Ireland.'

'How was it that your people afforded to send you to college then?'

'I had an uncle who died in America – my father's brother. He was a sergeant in the New York Police Department, killed in the line of duty. He didn't have any children and so he left what he had to me on the proviso that I used it to further my education. It wasn't very much. But it was enough to get me through most of my degree. Until the peelers crashed my digs, that was.'

'Were you close to your uncle?'

'He left for America when I was very young, so I don't really remember him. My father gave me a photo of him after we got news of his death. He was my father's younger brother.'

'He must have thought the world of you, though, to leave you the money for your education.'

'I think he had a sympathy for younger sons, being one himself. He knew my elder brother would probably inherit the farm.'

'It's strange, isn't it,' she said. 'How someone you barely know can love you so much. I haven't seen some of my nephews and nieces in years, since my brother emigrated to Glasgow, and they would hardly know me from Adam now, but my heart aches for them every day.'

Mrs Gleason made us a heap of bacon and eggs and we wolfed it down with tea and wheaten bread. I was feeling an awful lot happier since Peter had taken it upon himself to speak to O'Riordain. Eamon agreed. 'It'll be more of a conversation between officers rather than the upstart other-ranks pestering him.'

After a while Brendan joined us for a cup of tea and then Fiona returned from her shopping. She was a fine-looking young woman with fair hair, a chatty disposition and a lovely smile. I could see why she would drive a man away from the drink.

We lingered over breakfast so long that it was past lunchtime when we finally wandered back in the direction of McLaughlin's office. Peter was out and he had left no more instructions for us with Bronagh so we went into the kitchen and made ourselves tea. After letting it brew for a few minutes I poured out three cups. Eamon doctored them with milk and then lifted a mug and stomped off up the stairs to deliver it to Bronagh.

'You're right, Mick,' he said when he returned. 'She does have lovely dimples when she smiles.'

We spent much of the afternoon sipping tea. Then, as the darkness began to gather, we decided to repair to Toner's, because it had a fire and, frankly, neither of us had a fucking clue about what we should be doing next, apart from waiting for Peter.

The place was quiet enough and three-quarters empty when we got there. But we still occupied, as had become our habit, the snug in the back, and set up the chess set. It was my turn on white and I decided to try a queen's pawn opening to see if that would throw Eamon off. It didn't.

'Can I ask you a question, Mick?' he said after responding to my opening.

'Of course.'

'What's all this "rule of law" thing that Peter goes on about?'

'You don't understand what it means?'

'Well, I know what each of the words mean, but it's just that it seems to mean something else when he puts them together.'

'It's the idea that it is the law, properly administered, that governs a people, not the whims of any monarch or minister or mob, and that no one is above the law.'

'So when the mob gathers with flaming torches and pitchforks, or the minister wants rid of his mistress's husband on trumped-up charges, the law should protect the witch and the cuckold, and restrain the human excesses, or punish them when they transgress the law.'

'Exactly. It's an idea that is said to go back as far as Aristotle, who said "It is better for the law to rule than one of the citizens." They are wrong, though.'

'Who?'

'Them who says it was Aristotle's idea. It is at least a hundred years older. Sophocles dramatised the idea in *Oedipus Rex*, in which, as a result of the king's own investigation, he finds himself responsible for the plague on Thebes. He realises that he must be held accountable, just as anyone else would be, even though he is the king.'

'When did you find time to read Sophocles?'

'At school. There was a pretty decent library. It's how I knew about Agamemnon too.'

'What prompted you to read him, though?'

'Dirty stories are lean on the ground in South Armagh.'

'Sure that Cuchulainn fella was from your part of the world and he was a dirty bastard.'

'I'm afraid we were only ever allowed edited highlights of the Cattle Raid of Cooley. But from what I recall Ferdia, a Connaught man as you are well aware, was not the most chaste either, being bribed to try to kill his foster brother with gifts of women slaves, the body of the Queen's own daughter, and Queen Mebh herself if all that wasn't enough for him.'

'It was the fear of being cursed for dishonour for seven generations, at every hearth and fireside from West Connaught to South Ulster, that compelled Ferdia to fight Cuchulainn. The prospect of Borgian quantities of sex with dozens of women if he won was mere icing on the cake.'

'Well, for some reasons the Christian Brothers didn't object to dirty stories if they were from classical antiquity.'

'It must have thrown a bit of a spanner in your youthful reading pleasure when you discovered the bold Oedipus was fucking his ma.'

'That may have been why the Brothers allowed it. For the more delicately minded that could put you off for the rest of your life. But at least there was the Bible to remedy that problem.'

'What do you mean?'

'That Song of Songs is pretty racy. A proper antidote to all them dubious Greek shenanigans.'

'Aye. But that is stuff that you probably should keep out of the sweaty hands of sixteen-year-olds. All that talk of "kisses of the mouth" and "love better than wine". It would lead to a great danger of young fellas spontaneously combusting all over the place. Must cost a fortune to clean up.'

'None of that sort of thing going on in your school?'

'I'm sure there was. But I was so painfully shy at school, and so stretched academically to try to get a scholarship, that I did not do much reading around the curriculum. I really didn't start seriously reading until I was in the trenches with time on my hands.'

'You've made up for your late start it would seem.'

'Kind of you to say. Not being a pig-ignorant gobshite does take a bit of effort. But it is that effort that separates human beings from fanatics and zealots.'

After losing the first game I asked Eamon, 'Who taught you to play?' It had been on my mind for a while but I'd never got around to asking before.

'My da taught me the moves. But I got friendly with a fella from Tipperary when we were both in hospital in France at the end of 1914 and he gave me a crash course in strategy. There is a lot of waiting around in war, so there was plenty of time to practise after that. When I was in France I used to dream of getting back home and finally beating my da at chess, but of course he thwarted me again.'

'He upped his game?'

'No, the cunning bastard died before I got home.'

'Oh,' I said. 'Sorry.'

'Not to worry, Mick. It was a while ago now. Another game?'

'Aye. Shall we have a pint?'

'May as well, I suppose.'

I went to the bar while Eamon set up the board.

'Can I ask you something, Eamon?' I said as I sat back down.

'Go ahead.'

'Your opinion of O'Riordain.'

'The one about him being a cunt?'

'Aye, that one.'

'What about it?'

'It must once not have been so absolute?'

'Why do you reckon that?'

'He knew about your experiences of shooting prisoners. I wouldn't have thought that was something that you would have told everyone.'

Eamon took a slug of his pint. 'No, it's not. After I got back from France, Jack came to visit. Now I always thought he was a cunt from school days. He always wanted to be the big fellow and had a streak of the bully in him, liked to throw his weight around. But he can turn on the charm and he turned it on me. Said he could do with somebody of my experience to work with the Volunteers. I thought to myself, maybe he's changed. So we were friendly for a bit. Quite frankly, I liked having my opinion taken seriously, because I didn't leave the army with any illusions about the British Empire or their likelihood of keeping their promises for Home Rule once the war was over. So I felt it was a chance for me to put to some good use the stupidity of my swallowing their lies and false promises and joining up.'

'So you had a few heart to hearts with Jack over the years?'

'I suppose you could put it that way. I thought it was my patriotic duty to let Jack know what he would be up against if it came to another round of shooting.'

'That's why you told him about the murder of prisoners?'

'Aye, amongst other things, like tactics and training. Though I'm not sure how interested he was in those. I always felt he didn't drill the Volunteers hard enough.'

'But what happened at the police barracks made you change your mind about him?'

'It did. I actually think I might have forgiven Jack shooting those peelers. I could understand, empathise even, with the fury after a fight where you have lost some of your own. But it was the way he did it that bothered me, the way he made them dig their own graves first. That wasn't battle rage, that was cold-blooded sadism. It's a special kind of fucker for that sort of thing.'

'There's a lot of the greatest military leaders seem to have been that sort of fucker. Neither Julius Caesar nor Alexander were above putting defeated enemies to the sword, nor raping and plundering the civilian populations. Do you think it's ever possible to be a great war captain and a decent person?'

'I have wondered about that over the years. If it's not impossible, it's certainly very difficult. Military training is about teaching young men how to mutilate other young men. Battle is about putting that into practice, actually getting young men to mutilate other young men. If you look at the conduct of the war just past, the generals' jobs would have been impossible if they had cared at all about human life and human suffering. They lined us up like livestock and fed us into meat grinders for four bloody years. The casualties only bothered them insofar as it limited them lining us up for butchery somewhere else. But I could probably have forgiven them that if they had shown any sign that they knew what they were doing. But, when it was all over, those bloody old men returned to the loving embrace of their class and accepted the adulation of their nations for overseeing the culling of an entire generation of European youth.'

'Do you think we are going to be the same here? If we win this war, will Jack be the man of the moment, our own "perfect, gentle knight" to lead us in peacetime as in war?'

'That is a distinct possibility. Jack loves being the big man. And people really buy that noble warrior shite. Those who have never seen war tend to romanticise it as something brave and glorious. Or rather, they tend to romanticise the behaviour and actions of their own side. The enemy will always be accused of every degradation known to man, whereas one of "our boys", even if he descends to the level of eviscerating children, will nevertheless be regarded as a hero. And for those of us who have been through war and know the truth of it, well, we are not going to share that truth with the uninitiated. And amongst the initiated we will value courage and comradeship above humanity to the enemy. Or put another way, the plain people of Mayo will conveniently forget the cries for mercy from those police before they were murdered, and those who helped Jack murder them will be bound to him for ever by ties of blood.'

'You don't fit in either of those categories. He must regard you then as one enormous pain in the arse.'

'I don't think he regards me as anything at all, to be honest.'

'But he did just offer you a transfer to a flying column?'

'That's probably just soft-soap shite. There's as much chance of him seeing that through as there is of me marrying a Russian princess. I think he just wanted something from us, but fuck knows what. No, he has boxed me up nicely where I am, as unfit to serve, and no doubt discredits me further with a few well-placed words doubting my full loyalty to the Republic, given my prior service to the king.'

'I don't think Peter buys that oul shite.'

'No, but he's but one man. And after a war, the people of Ireland in their dubious wisdom will be fetishising the soldiers and killers in just the same way as the British so routinely do to their own, irrespective of what horrors they perpetrated in the name of their empire. For all his strengths, Peter is not a warrior. Unfortunately, it's the blood sacrifice that tends to rouse the masses, not the exhortation to uphold rule of law or take care of each other, as Peter would like.'

'That's a bleak thought,' I said. 'And to think I only got involved in the hope it would impress girls.'

Eamon laughed. 'Ach, we've all been there,' he said, and moved a pawn. 'How's that working out for you?'

'Not as well as I hoped. When all is said and done, I think girls would generally prefer a fella who can dance than some eejit whose only distinction is a commitment to national independence and the social revolution. And fellas like that are ten a penny at the moment.'

'Don't give up hope, Mick. You're not a bad-looking fella and you've read a few books. As we speak there is someone out there who is searching for the very virtues you possess. And if there isn't, I can promise you from my own experience that women seem to lower their standards quite drastically as they get older.'

'Really?'

'Indeed! At eighteen they may be dreaming of some Adonis with a fine singing voice and a nimble footwork. At twenty-six they can be swayed by the mere prospect of a British Army pension.'

'That's a bit cynical.'

"Tis not. It's hopeful. It's a hopeful thought that someday some woman who you may think is beyond your wildest dreams might just fall in love with you and you really will have no idea why. And if she ever tells you it will probably be a complete surprise to you what it is.'

'Did your wife ever tell you what it was about you that made her choose you?'

'Well, I still like to believe my good looks and erudition had something to do with it. But her story, and she stuck to it through thick and thin, was that it was my terrible French. She said it showed I was prepared to make an effort. And, I suppose, my terrible accent granted me the distinction of being a curiosity on the streets of Paris.'

'You didn't fancy staying on in Paris after the war?'

'You can't get a decent cup of tea in Paris.'

'You couldn't learn to love coffee?'

'Ach, to be honest, after four years of blood and mud I just wanted to go home. And Paris wasn't that for me any more after Juliette died.'

'Did you know you would be coming back to another war?'

'I thought that there would be trouble after the 1916 executions. Then I knew there would be after Dáil Éireann established itself in Dublin. I was just hoping I could stay out of it. But in my heart I knew that was a foolish idea, particularly after the first time I saw Shamey O'Neill parading with a gun. There is a dimwit, if ever there was one, desperate for a blood-soaked crusade against everyone different or who he doesn't understand. That, and I had kicked the shite out of him at school once and I don't think he's the sort who would place his sacred duty of defending the Republic over a squalid opportunity to even a few scores if he saw the chance. That's about the only thing I respect about the little gobshite.'

'Why did you kick the shite out of him?'

'Fucked if I can remember. But I'm pretty sure he deserved it anyway.'

We played a couple more games over the next hour or so, moving only occasionally from the snug to have a piss or to resupply ourselves with slowly sipped pints.

After a while we heard a murmur of subdued commotion from the public bar, heard the cadence of a woman's voice cut through the male murmuring, and then footsteps approaching. We stood up, and as we did so Eamon picked up his Webley that had been sitting on the table between us, stuffed it into his belt at the small of his back and smoothed his jacket back down.

The door to the snug opened before we managed to get either of our hands to it and standing there was Laoise, Dr Hennessy's receptionist.

'I've been looking for ye,' she said. 'I just come from McLaughlin's. Bronagh said to try here.'

We resumed our seats in the snug and Eamon said, 'Well, what can we do for you? Do you want to sit down? I think Toner has some sherry in the back if you would like a drink?'

'Sherry?' she said, not bothering to hide the disgust and incredulity in her voice. 'What do you think this is? The nineteenth century?'

Eamon managed no more than, 'Em…'

'Anyway, I'm not here for a drink,' she said. 'I've just come to bring you a message.'

'Well,' said Eamon. 'Fire ahead.'

'It's from Dr Hennessy. She asked me to ask the two of you if you could drop round to see her this evening at about seven.'

'In the surgery?' I asked.

'No,' she said. 'At her house.'

Eamon and I looked at each other, I am not sure which of us was more surprised. Then Eamon said, 'Aye, grand. Tell her we'll drop over round seven.'

'I will so,' said Laoise. 'All the best.' And with that she turned and marched out of the pub.

We looked at each other. 'Have you spoken to her since yesterday?' I asked Eamon.

'I haven't,' said Eamon, 'and I was just about to ask you the same thing.'

'I haven't either,' I said and we both fell silent. 'Maybe,' I suggested, 'she has realised our fundamental perspicacity and nobility of purpose since yesterday and wants to be reconciled with us.'

'I thought you told me your da was a pig farmer, Mick.'

'He was. But what's that got to do with anything?'

'I think he would have mentioned the existence of flying pigs before now, don't you?'

XXVI

We cycled up to Dr Hennessy's house just before seven. The splatter of rain had turned into something a bit more persistent and the wind was still raw.

We parked our bikes against the wall of the house, out of the wind, and knocked on the front door. Dr Hennessy answered it with a lamp in her hand and her hair loose, just as she had when we visited on Tuesday, but this time more formally dressed. 'Come on in,' she said.

'Down in the kitchen again, Doctor?' asked Eamon.

'Not this evening,' she said and instead led us through a door opposite the library where she had taken us on our previous visit.

The door led into a comfortable sitting room, already brightly lit with lamps. There already, on the sofa with a very large glass of whiskey in his fist and a sheen of sweat on his forehead, was Father Martin Crosby.

'This is something of a surprise,' said Eamon.

'Sit down would you please, Eamon. You too, Mick,' said Dr Hennessy. We complied.

'Can I get you boys something to drink?' she asked.

'Whiskey, I suppose,' said Eamon.

'Aye. Me too,' I said.

Dr Hennessy poured us generous measures from a cut-glass decanter on a side table. As she sorted out the drinks, Eamon and Crosby never took their eyes off each other. I, however, took the opportunity to have a proper, uninterrupted stare at Dr Hennessy as she bent over the table, her copper hair shimmering in the lamp light. She was one of those women who seemed to glow on her own, and I imagined for a moment that even in darkness she would still have lit the place up with the luminescence of her skin and the sea-green glitter of her eyes.

Jesus, I had it bad.

'So what is this all about?' asked Eamon, once we had our drinks.

'Martin has something to tell you,' said Dr Hennessy. 'Isn't that right, Martin?'

Crosby said nothing but nodded, and then took a large slug of his whiskey.

'Martin, is it?' asked Eamon.

'It is my name,' said Crosby.

'Well?' said Eamon. 'What is it you want to get off your chest?'

'You must understand how difficult this is for me,' said Crosby.

'We might,' said Eamon, 'if we had any notion what "this" was.'

'When you came to see me yesterday you deduced, correctly, that I already knew Liam had been murdered.'

'Aye, and you told us you knew because Dr Hennessy had told you about the results of her medical examination of Liam's body.'

'Yes. Sophia did come to see me after the examination, and she did tell me what she had found.'

'Yes?'

'But I already knew Liam had been murdered.'

138

I felt the blood drain out of my head and the room began to spin. If I hadn't already been sitting I would have had to. I noticed Eamon. His head snapped back as if he had been hit with a jab to his chin. Only Dr Hennessy remained composed. She knew, I thought.

After what seemed like an interminable pause, Eamon managed two words: 'Go on.'

Crosby took another shot of whiskey. 'He came to see me shortly after I got back from Castlebar. I was making tea in the parochial house when I heard a rap at the door. He said to me, "Father, I wish to confess." So I brought him inside to the parlour and he told me his story.

'He said he had arranged to meet Liam after Mass. He had said to him that he would give him a few bob if he was able to run some messages for him. I know Liam had started saving up because he wanted to be a teacher – that's what all of the extra hours at Bruton's was about. You've seen his family's place. They would have been hard-pushed to put him to secondary school, let alone training college, scholarship or not, so he was trying to help out. You were right also when you discerned I had a particular affection for the lad. He was a lovely youngster, but he had guts and ambition and idealism too. He wanted to make the world a better place. If I could have had a son I would have liked him to be like Liam.'

There were tears running down Crosby's face. Dr Hennessy took a handkerchief from her sleeve and passed it to him. He set down his whiskey glass for a moment and wiped his face. He was quiet for a while longer as he tried to get control of himself again. Finally, he picked up the glass, took another mouthful of whiskey, and continued.

'He told me he had prepared for Liam before he arrived. With the two of them alone the rest wasn't difficult. A grown man overpowering a ten-year-old child. He tied his wrists together and gagged him, then stripped and raped him. When he had finished that he strangled him, dressed him again, and then used his vehicle to dispose of the body.'

Crosby tried to take another drink but discovered his glass was empty. Dr Hennessy stood up, retrieved the decanter and refilled his glass.

'Who?' said Eamon.

'You know that breaking the seal of confession under any circumstances results in automatic excommunication.'

'Father, there are a lot of reasons in what you say that make me disbelieve you. Your sudden scruples about canon law are not among them.'

'Like what?'

'You say you loved Liam like a son. But here is a fellow comes to your home to tell you he killed the child in the most horrendous and sadistic of ways and your reaction was to listen to what he had to say, give him absolution, and send him on his way, no doubt with the exhortation to sin no more?'

'I have told you what he said, not how I reacted.'

'Enlighten us please, Father.'

There was a glint of steel from Crosby. 'For a start, I did not give him absolution.'

'No?'

'No. I told him I prayed he would roast in hell for all eternity.'

'Isn't that against the rules?' asked Eamon.

'Since when have you become so interested in canon law?'

'Just trying to understand what happened.'

'Well, if you were my bishop or confessor I would say that I felt there was a sound theological basis for my refusal of absolution.'

'And what was that?'

'I didn't think he was properly disposed towards the sacrament.'

'What does that even mean?' asked Eamon.

'It means I thought he was taking the piss,' said Crosby.

'So how did he take all that?'

'When he told me first what he had done I didn't believe it. He didn't mention a name, just what he had done. Then as the details started to convince me, the dread grew and I asked the question, "Who?" When he told me I went for him. I tried to kill him with my bare hands, but he got the better of me and put me down. He was laughing when he left.'

'Were there any other reasons, apart from the details of the killing, that made you believe him?'

'You must understand that I have been this man's confessor for some years.'

'I presumed that,' said Eamon.

'There were things that he had told me before.'

'Jaysus, this is like pulling teeth,' said Eamon. 'Like what?'

'He had been abused by his father from an early age. This had rather shaped his sexual preferences.'

'For boys?'

'For violence. He had previously confessed violent and violent sexual acts going as far back as his adolescence.'

'Did he tell you about his abuse in confession?' I asked.

'He did. He seemed to be under the impression that he needed absolution for that as well.'

We all fell silent again. I took a swallow of the whiskey and became suddenly aware of the loud ticking of Dr Hennessy's grandmother clock on the mantelpiece.

'So why have you decided to tell us this now?'

'After you spoke to Sophia yesterday she came to me and told me she was concerned that you thought I had killed Liam.'

'Ah,' said Eamon. 'This is sort of what I expected. You have begun to worry about your own skin, so you have decided on a cunning ruse to throw us off the scent.'

'No. After you two eejits have singularly failed to bring the perpetrator of this monstrosity to any semblance of justice, I have become concerned that he will be left free to roam and prey upon other defenceless children.'

'Didn't they teach you to trust in God in the seminary?' Eamon asked.

'Maybe that is what I should be doing,' said Crosby. 'But after millions butchered across Europe for no discernible purpose these past few years, God does seem to be acting like a bit of a useless cunt at the moment.'

'So instead you are trusting in us?'

'That is the sorry state of affairs in which we find ourselves.'

'And so you risk excommunication.'

'I studied moral philosophy in the seminary. It was my favourite subject. I even thought of doing a doctorate in it.

So believe me when I tell you that when I weigh that risk of my own excommunication against the life of a child it is as a feather against a lead weight. But,' he said with sudden intensity, 'I am also human. And I do, with a passion I have never felt before, wish that bastard to roast in hell for all eternity. And the sooner that can begin, the better I would like it.'

Crosby's words reverberated in the silence. 'So,' Eamon said. 'Who?'

Crosby took another swig of the whiskey and said nothing.

'Come on, Martin, for fuck sake,' Eamon said. 'You are plainly no stranger to mortal sin. What's another one between the four of us?'

'What do you mean?' Dr Hennessy asked.

'Really, Doctor? It was clear from the intensity with which you defended Father Crosby during our conversation yesterday that you had a particular regard for his reverence here. However, I did not know until this evening that you were actually lovers.'

I wanted to shout, 'What?' but I managed to keep my gob shut. Dr Hennessy instead filled the silence with a different question: 'How…?' she said. The rest of her words died away, but it was enough.

Eamon said, 'I told you I was married once. I understand the level of trust that can bring. If you are going to contemplate committing a mortal sin, whether that is breaking the seal of confession, or framing an innocent for murder, it is not something that you are ever going to do with a casual woman friend or a passing fancy. You would only do that with someone you trust absolutely. Being totally naked before someone else, being inside them and sharing blood and intimacy, that will do it, though.'

Dr Hennessy blushed slightly, but not for long. 'Fuck it,' she said. 'It's true. I've never understood this fucking celibacy rule. If Martin had had the decency to be Church of Ireland, I would be a vicar's wife by now. So let me be clear as someone who knows Martin, and, appositely, I do mean that in the Biblical sense, there is no way this man could hurt a child. Specifically, there is no way he could have hurt this child. I know how much he loved Liam.'

Eamon and I looked at each other. Then I looked at Crosby who was looking intently at Dr Hennessy. I couldn't help feeling jealous. 'Lucky bastard,' I thought and an image of Sophia naked, with her porcelain skin and her copper hair unbound, came into my mind uninvited but with a startling, vivid clarity. I tried to shake it out of my head.

'So,' said Eamon. 'The key question remains unanswered. Who?'

Crosby took another drink. 'Martin?' said Dr Hennessy.

I knew what Crosby was going to say before he said it. We both did. It still hit us with a force of terror.

'Jack O'Riordain,' he said.

'Fuck,' I said.

It was Eamon's turn to drink some whiskey. He was silent for some moments before he spoke again. 'Even if we were to believe you,' he said, 'I do not imagine that you would be prepared to offer this testimony up in a court of law.'

'What courts? With the IRA running riot across the west and south there is no justice system any more.'

'And yet here we sit. Irish Republican Police in service to a courts system, legally constituted by the democratically elected parliament of the Irish people.'

'The same court system that passed sentence on those poor men at the police barracks?'

'Is that what you thought was going to happen? We'd say thanks for that, Father. We'll just take Jack O'Riordain out now to the nearest ditch and blow his brains out?'

'That has become something of a *modus operandi* of your lot in these parts,' said Dr Hennessy.

'I must tell you both that even before I got a gut full of killing in the trenches, I was opposed to the death penalty. Mick here, being an enlightened young socialist, is, I understand, of the same opinion.'

I nodded my agreement.

'That must make things a bit awkward being in the IRA.'

'Indeed, there are tensions. But not in this particular instance. Military matters are beyond the realm of the Dáil courts. But this is not a military matter. It is Mr McLaughlin's intention to try to bring this case to the first sitting of the Western circuit in Ballina at the end of this month.'

'And for that we need evidence,' I chipped in. 'And even if you were prepared to testify, I cannot see the court looking favourably on the word of a priest with such contempt for his vows.' That came out a bit more vehemently than I had hoped. I suppose jealousy does that to a man.

Crosby looked directly at me. 'Sometimes you just fall in love,' he said.

'Aye,' said Eamon, coming to the rescue. 'I know what you

mean. But that doesn't alter Mick's central point. The solid citizens of Connaught would not look favourably on a priest who has so singularly failed in his celibacy vows. And with a red-headed Protestant to boot! You would be lucky if you got away with excommunication after that. You'd probably be stoned to death by those hard-faced fuckers out of sheer envy, if nothing else.'

Crosby took a sip of his whiskey. 'Frankly,' he said, 'I wasn't sure what I expected would happen next. I just know O'Riordain has to be stopped. I think he is getting a taste for it now, for murder.'

'We'll speak to Peter and see if he has any ideas.'

'What will you say?' asked Crosby.

'Now that is a good point,' said Eamon. 'He is a very sincere Catholic, is Peter, and, even though he is a man of the world, he would be shocked and horrified to hear that you have had carnal knowledge of Sophia here – can I call you Sophia? I think we have gone past formalities now, don't you?'

Sophia nodded.

'As I was saying, Peter would be appalled at the weakness of the flesh you have shown, let alone the breaking of the seal of confession. So perhaps we will just tell him we have been reflecting on Jack as a suspect and think we should have a closer look at him after all.'

'Peter was meant to be meeting O'Riordain today,' I added. 'He is a shrewd enough man. Perhaps his suspicions will be roused.'

'That is, of course, if you are telling the truth, Martin. Don't believe for a second that just because we are looking at O'Riordain again we have swallowed whole your story.'

Crosby nodded. 'Okay so,' said Crosby. 'I'll leave it with youse for a bit then.'

Silence descended on us. I sipped my whiskey and looked at Eamon who was doing the same, looking at me evenly across the rim of his glass. I wondered what he was thinking and I hoped he made more sense of the situation than I did. I was still reeling. One question came to me though.

'Why do you think he picked Liam?' I asked.

Crosby looked at me for a moment. 'I don't know. Liam hero-worshipped Jack. Said once he would like to be like him. All the glamour of being an IRA battalion commander, I suppose. I think Jack is one of the reasons Liam wanted to become a teacher. Maybe Jack realised the power that he had over Liam and saw that he could use that to draw him into his trap.'

'His dreams got him killed so?' I asked.

'Just like thousands of other Irish people cramming them-selves onto coffin ships in the hope of a better life in America,' said Eamon.

'Or like every woman who has ever been raped or murdered by someone they loved and trusted,' said Sophia.

Crosby emptied his glass and then wiped his face again with the handkerchief that Sophia had given him. 'I'd best be off,' he said. 'I've got an early start tomorrow morning.'

He stood, followed by Sophia. 'Us too,' said Eamon, and lifted himself from his chair.

I heaved myself slowly to my feet, feeling the whiskey, and the four of us, led by Sophia, moved towards the door. She turned the handle and then hesitated. She turned back to us. 'Can I ask you two boys to be discreet about what you have learned here, please. I mean, what you said about people's attitudes towards Martin will be doubly true for me, what with me being a woman.'

'And a Protestant,' said Eamon. 'And worst of all a ginger! Rarely has there been such a perfect candidate for the role of Scarlet Woman in all of Mayo.'

'Please,' she said, and she wasn't smiling.

'Don't worry, Sophia,' he said. 'I think it's fair to say that the two of us have a proper detestation of informers. So neither of us are given to blabbing.'

'Thank you. Really, thank you,' she said and she clasped each of our hands in turn in both of hers. They were cool and dry when they touched me, but I still felt a jolt of electricity in the contact.

We followed the passage to the back of the house, towards the kitchen door. Crosby, it turned out, had brought his car with him and, I presumed out of the habit of the secret lover, parked it at the back of the house. The wind was picking up and lashing the rain with the force of hailstones.

'Can I give you boys a lift?' he asked.

'Kind of you,' said Eamon, 'but we are going to need our bicycles first thing in the morning.'

'You could stay here if you want,' said Sophia.

It wasn't the first time in the evening we were surprised. 'I have the spare room made up if you two fellows don't mind sharing a bed.'

We looked at each other and we looked at the rain. Then I said, 'That would be very kind of you, Doctor.'

'Sophia,' she said.

'Sophia.'

Crosby nodded farewell to Sophia. It was a chaste enough farewell given what we had learned over the course of this evening's conversation. A habit born of the nature of their relationship, I presumed. Then he pulled his overcoat around him and ran to his car through the rain. He started the engine and waved to us through the windscreen as he started down the drive.

Sophia closed the door. 'I'll just show you boys where you'll sleep, and then I will make you something to eat.'

'That's very kind of you, Doc,' said Eamon.

'Not a bother. It'll just be sandwiches.'

'Ham?' I asked.

'If we're lucky,' she said and she led us up the stairs, lamp in hand.

XXVII

'So, how long have you and his reverence been this sordid and shameful item?'

Eamon didn't believe in beating around the bush. Sophia had barely sat herself down at her kitchen table having served us tea and set out the bread, ham, cheese and butter for us to help ourselves, but she didn't miss a beat.

'There is nothing sordid and shameful about us, you cheeky little bastard,' she said.

'You know, Doc, for a prospective vicar's wife, you've quite the colourful vocabulary.'

Sophia lit up a cigarette. 'I suppose,' she said. 'Hanging out with all those suffragettes in my Dublin youth taught me some awful language. But I could have developed worse habits.'

'What like?' I asked.

'Like holding my fucking tongue.'

Eamon grinned at that. 'So go on then. What's the story about you and Marty?'

I was relieved to see that Sophia didn't seem to be taking offence, or if she was she was hiding it well.

'Why do you want to know? Does it give you some sort of vicarious thrill?'

'I wouldn't put it quite like that. I suppose I'm just nosy.'

'Maybe you are cut out to be a detective after all, then.'

'I'll take that as a sort of a compliment,' said Eamon. 'So go on.'

Sophia said nothing for a moment and took a drag of her cigarette.

'My husband was killed on the Somme in July 1916. Were you there?'

'Only at the later stages of the battle. Thankfully I missed the first days.'

'Well, people were polite enough, but in the aftermath of the Dublin rebellion I don't think they were feeling that sympathetic towards the widow of a British officer.'

'But Martin was different.'

'He was. He didn't let politics get in the way of our friendship. And then it became something more after the New Year.'

'A beautifully simple love story. If only St Augustine had not been so hung up on matters of the flesh.'

'Aye, such a stupid fucking rule that, clerical celibacy. How do you understand and guide people on the most fundamental element of family life if you do not live it? But it's worse than that,' she went on, 'remember what it was like when you were an adolescent. All those raging hormones and no outlet. Was there anything you thought about more than sex? What it would be like? Who it would be with? How it would feel?'

'Aye,' said Eamon, 'I'm not sure I was ever able to turn my mind usefully to anything else until after I met Juliette and she put me out of my misery.'

'Indeed, it's them who don't have sex who are most obsessed by it. So it must be agony for the Catholic bishops of Ireland, like being perpetually fourteen. Ignoring everything else that is important because of this one overwhelming obsession.'

I said nothing. I would rather not listen to this, because I was beginning to feel like an embarrassed fourteen-year-old again myself, not helped by an image that had crept into my head of Sophia unbuttoning her blouse for her lover in some lamplit room before a brass bed.

I decided to try to steer the conversation somewhere a little less intimate.

'Why was the Somme such carnage?' I asked.

'Do you understand the term "non-sequitur", Mick?' asked Eamon.

'It's not a non-sequitur,' I said. 'This is the first chance I have had to get a word in edgeways.'

Eamon smiled. 'Fair enough,' he said. 'Well, the British generals would like you to believe that it was because the Germans put a dent in their plans by attacking Verdun, and forcing the French to withdraw their forces from the offensive they had agreed with the British. But the ground at the Somme was awful for attacking troops, the Germans were well dug in, and our brilliant generals had not worked out what was the best way to fight against such entrenched positions.'

'What is the best way to fight against such positions?' I asked.

'Wait for the Americans,' said Sophia.

Eamon let out a loud snort of laughter at that. 'I never took you for a military strategist, Doctor.'

'You forget, I've been reading *War and Peace*,' she said. 'And when war takes the most important person in the world from you, it does deepen one's interest in the whole sorry mess.'

'Aye,' said Eamon. 'War does that. It consumes not only life, but love itself.'

'But here you are again, part of another war, inflicting on others what you have had to endure yourself.'

'What do you mean?'

'Francis Harris.'

'Who was he?'

'Perhaps better known in these parts as Police Constable Harris.'

'He was killed at the barracks?'

'He was. Nobody has ever told me if he was killed in the fight or murdered after.'

'I doubt if anyone knows. No one was taking names.'

'He had been married three months. Was waiting for a transfer to a married posting.'

'How are you so well informed on this?'

'His wife came to see me a few weeks ago, after she got news of what happened here. I know you are as familiar with grief as I am, Eamon, but that never makes it any easier a thing to witness.'

'I tried to stop those killings,' said Eamon.

'But you didn't succeed. And if someone hadn't set light to the roof of the barracks those final killings might not ever have happened.'

Eamon was silent.

'It was you did that, I heard,' said Sophia.

'It was necessary,' said Eamon.

'Necessary why?'

'To take the barracks. To remove the eyes and ears of the British from these parts. To establish the authority of the Republic.'

'Well, I'm not sure what sort of authority you are talking about, Eamon, but the moral authority of the Republic was rather badly tarnished as a result of what happened once those poor policemen surrendered, don't you think?'

'I did not think Jack was going to kill the prisoners.'

'But he did. Him and your comrades. And you made it all possible.'

'Aye,' said Eamon. 'In more ways than one probably. But we were all helped along to that sordid moment by the righteousness of our cause.'

'I suppose that is why they say the road to hell is paved with good intentions. It does tend to be the righteous who are most comfortable standing in mortal judgement over others, forgetting the log in their own eyes as they obsess over the specks in the eyes of others. I imagine the Kaiser thought he was being righteous when he unleashed his armies on Europe, just as the English felt they were being righteous as they butchered themselves an empire from the lives of people who had never done them any harm. Maybe if the more timorous amongst us were in charge there would be less bloodshed. You know the sort, the ones who when they see the failings of others are reminded of their own failings instead of passing judgement.'

'You may be right,' said Eamon, 'but it's difficult to see how we might get to that utopia without reducing the British Empire, and all like it, to ashes and dust.'

'Therein lies the paradox,' said Sophia, 'because in the process we may end up transforming ourselves into the very thing we wish to destroy.' She sipped her tea. 'I've never been in battle,' she said, 'so I can only imagine the courage it took to do what you did, exposing yourself under fire, I understand?'

Eamon said nothing, so she continued, 'But look at the consequences: murdered prisoners; widows and orphans. What sort of people do you think you will be after all of this is over? War destroys more than life and love. It also corrupts wisdom and courage, as the best aspects of people are reduced to the elemental purpose of slaughtering our fellow human beings.'

'But what other options do we have? You think the British are going to leave here without a fight? The sort of them they have no respect for anyone who are not as bloody and warlike as themselves. Every peaceful effort towards justice for this country over the past hundred years they have ignored or destroyed. Even your own suffragettes were driven to direct action in the end.'

'Indeed,' said Sophia. 'But I'd hardly put smashing a few windows in the same moral category as putting bullets into the brains of human beings. And anyway, it's not just the British you are fighting here, is it? This war is already a civil one. In the north, neighbours are turning on each other in the most vicious ways imaginable, as you must be well aware, Mick. And Francis Harris was from Clare, twenty-three years old and dreaming of his whole life in front of him with his pregnant wife. So even when the grief fades the bitterness won't.'

We were silent. 'This war is making a mockery of the Irish flag itself,' she said.

'How so?' I asked.

'Green, white and orange it is, representing Nationalist and Unionist, Catholic and Protestant, the nation complete only when those two traditions are united in peace. Instead this war pits the two against each other in a way that will be remembered with bitterness for generations.'

She got up from the table and walked to a cupboard. She opened it and took out a bottle of whiskey and three glasses. She returned to the table with them and sloshed out three measures. She swallowed her whiskey in one gulp and then refilled her glass.

'You know I heard some gobshite in my surgery the other day referring to the Irish flag as "green, white and gold". No notion what the flag is meant to represent. That whole ideal of uniting Catholic, Protestant and Dissenter under the common name of Irish already abandoned before the Republic has even properly established itself.'

Sophia took a cigarette from a packet that was sitting on the table, lit it, breathed in and exhaled a long cloud of smoke.

'Why do you bother giving us the time of day,' I asked, 'if that is what you feel?'

She took another drag on her cigarette.

'You said a couple of days ago you didn't know why my husband, Charlie, joined the British Army, Eamon.'

'I did.'

'It was much the same reason as yourself. He joined it because it's what our parliamentary leadership recommended to secure Ireland's future. Bizarre as it may seem, he thought there may be some opportunity to break down our own sectarianism if we, Catholic, Protestant and Dissenter, confronted German militarism together in the name of all the small nations of Europe. Charlie was as committed a Nationalist as you are. And I as much as he. But I do not believe that war can ever be the way to unite the people of this island.'

'That doesn't quite answer my question,' I said.

'It's part of an answer. I mean that I'm not as unsympathetic to you politically as you might have thought.'

'Well, what's the rest of the answer?' I asked.

'Liam Finnegan,' she said.

'What do you mean by that?' I asked.

'As I was tidying up that child's body for his parents, I couldn't help but imagine what he had been through in those last hours of his life, and I despaired that whoever had done that to him would ever be brought to justice. Then when you two showed up at my house on Tuesday evening I must admit that I was surprised that you had sustained an interest in what had happened longer than your latest hangover. So while you may never worry Scotland Yard with your investigative skills, your persistence did confirm a certain suspicion I had about your moral integrity.'

'Damned with faint praise,' said Eamon.

'You think that?' said Sophia. 'It was not my intention. You know as the doctor here I hear all sorts.'

'What like?'

'Well, I treated some of your wounded comrades after the fight at the barracks. One was a particularly obnoxious fucker, thought himself quite the wit.'

'Shamey O'Neill?' I asked.

'That was him. Slight injury to the hand, which I cleaned and bandaged. Anyway, he kept referring to Eamon here as "Hague Conventions Gleason".'

Eamon said nothing. 'The last leave Charlie had before he was killed,' Sophia continued, 'he told me some of what it was like in the trenches. He mentioned the raiding parties he had been on, sneaking into the German trenches to shoot them up at night, maybe capture a prisoner or two for intelligence gathering, but rarely much to show for it apart from a few dead or mutilated young men. I asked him, could he not refuse to participate? Charlie was a thoughtful and principled man and he admitted that it troubled him greatly too. But he worried also that any sort of protest would mark him out as a coward. He said he didn't have enough courage for that.'

'We've all been in that place. The shame of it has never left me,' said Eamon.

'I saw how that diminished my husband. I think at the end he wondered if the violence he had sought to oppose was not, perhaps, significantly less than that which he found himself a party to.'

We drank our whiskey in silence for a bit, and Sophia topped up our glasses again.

'You know, I haven't spoken about my husband in such a long time.'

'You miss him still?' I asked.

'Of course. I don't think I'll ever stop missing him. But I did wonder that last time we were together if I had lost him already. It was not just the moral compromises that diminished him, it was the killing itself. He told me about a German boy he had killed, shot as the boy was trying to bayonet him. It was unquestionably self-defence, he said, but I think it bothered him to the day he died, ending a life that had barely begun. He wondered had the young fella ever even seen a naked woman in the flesh, let alone made love to one.'

I felt myself blushing again, and hoped the relative gloom of the kitchen hid the redness of my face.

'Even just wars are evil,' said Eamon. 'The best you can hope for is that you can avoid the worst excesses of it.'

'But at the barracks you didn't just avoid the worst excesses,' Sophia said. 'You stood up for something better, a higher ideal. You tried to stop murder.'

'I'm hardly a moral paragon, Doctor. To my shame I've been complicit in similar things in France. So it turned my stomach to see it happening again. Half my problem is a general inability to keep my gob shut when I am annoyed.'

'Well, try not to keep your gob shut next time as well. Moral outrage is a particular type of courage, and that sort of courage can eventually become contagious. And that, I believe, more than even just war and killing, is what ultimately changes the world for the better.'

XXVIII

Sophia's spare room had a big brass bed that bore a striking resemblance to the one she had been undressing herself beside in my imagination.

The bed seemed to me to be bigger than the entire outhouse that I slept in at the Bonners'. She had also been thoughtful enough to light us a fire. It was without doubt the most luxurious accommodation I had ever stayed in.

We took our boots off and sat, top to tail, on the bed, Eamon smoking a cigarette. He had insisted that his greater age and military seniority give him the privilege of the choice of sides, and so now rested his head on a bolster piled against the headboard.

'So what did you make of all that then?' I asked.

'I'll say one thing,' said Eamon. ''Tis not often you get to hear a priest's confession.'

'Did you believe him?'

'I don't know. I am a little less suspicious of the fucker now I know he is skewering the doc.'

'The depths of your prejudices are really quite shallow, aren't they?'

'Them's the only sort of prejudices that are in any way morally defensible,' said Eamon. 'There may be some private amusement to be gained from considering Limerick a place filled with moral degenerates, or to suggest that Germans are a humourless bunch of Teutonics. But at the end of the day we are all human. If you are open to that fact it tends to demolish every prejudice once we're exposed to it.'

'Even with Dubs?'

'I'm not sure I have enough evidence on that one yet.'

'But you are prepared to consider Crosby in a less accusatory light?'

'I've thought about this a bit,' said Eamon. 'There are two things I am pretty sure you can say about all human beings: that they want to be loved and that they do not want to die. I can relate to Martin a bit more now that I see he is not immune to the allure of high cheekbones and a great arse.'

'She's smart and accomplished too, and she seems like a kind person.'

'I know that,' said Eamon. 'I was just highlighting the less obvious points.'

'You think priests have a particular weakness for the gingers?'

'You know, I have never thought about that,' said Eamon. 'Why do you ask?'

'All them Botticellis. A load of them were painted for clerical patrons.'

'Hmm,' Eamon mused. 'Where did you see them?'

'Books in the university library in Galway.'

'Weren't you meant to be studying law?'

'Hell is a place where the only reading material is tort and contracts.'

'Well, in answer to your question: 'Tis said that Mary Magdalene was a redhead, so I suppose the clergy may feel they are truly following the ways of our Lord and Saviour by a certain penchant for the gingers.'

Eamon took a drag on his cigarette, and then stubbed it out on an ashtray that rested in his lap. 'You liked her too, didn't you?' he said.

For a second I thought of denying it, but then I thought why bother. 'Aye,' I said. 'Green eyes.'

'Aye,' he said, 'I've heard tell that all green-eyed women are witches, so you had no fecking chance. Even with the less supernatural variety of women, eyes is a terror. It's how women steal your heart away, twinkling them things when they smile and then you're lost for ever.'

'You sound like you speak from experience.'

'Juliette,' he said. 'My wife.'

'She was a green-eyed woman?'

'Black eyes, the colour of sin.'

'Ah,' I said. 'So the moral of the story is what's for you won't go by you?'

'No. What's for you can go by you if you don't grasp the opportunity quick and hold onto it for what your life is worth. But, if you're a bit lucky, you might get more than one chance before you die.'

'I suspect if I, or anyone else for that matter, was to make an attempt to grab onto Dr Hennessy without her explicit say so, I'd end up pretty sharpish with a face like a scalped arse.'

'Aye,' said Eamon, 'that's a truth there is no getting away from. And it's difficult to contend with the tang of forbidden fruit. But the sea is teeming.'

Eamon lifted the ashtray from his lap and set it beneath the lamp on the bedside table.

'Some day, Mick, we'll go to the Louvre and have a look at their Botticellis together. I'm sure they have some pictures of naked blondes and brunettes too, take your mind off how your heart was bruised and battered during a small war in the County Mayo.'

Eamon leaned over to the bedside lamp. 'You ready?' he asked.

'Aye,' I said. Eamon blew out the lamp and the darkness descended on us.

'That school of hard knocks you went to,' I said.

'What about it?'

'It seems to have been pretty good. Maybe I should try to study there once I have finished with law in Galway.'

'I've some news for you Mick. You're already halfway through the master's course.'

SATURDAY

XXIX

THE NEXT MORNING we woke early and did our best to clean ourselves and tidy up the room. Sophia was down in the kitchen before us and had made us tea. She offered toast too, but we politely declined. We were both keen to see Peter.

The worst of the storm had passed and we cycled over to Peter's house at a brisk rate. Peter was away.

'Any thoughts where he might be, Eamon?' I asked.

'If we are lucky, he will have gone into the office to do a bit of work. If we are unlucky he will be gone to the races.'

We turned our bikes towards town and cycled to his office. The door was locked and there was no signs of habitation.

'Fuck,' said Eamon.

'Indeed,' I said, and got off my bike and leaned it against the wall.

We perched ourselves on the edge of the windowsill of McLaughlin's office and Eamon lit a cigarette. 'So what should we do now?' I asked.

'Fucked if I know,' he said. 'Anything from your lawyer training?'

'Nothing useful,' I said. 'I don't suppose it would be a good idea to interview Jack?'

'Not until we are sure that Peter has squared it off with him.'

'But if Crosby is telling the truth then I can't see him taking that quietly.'

'Sufficient unto the day is the evil thereof,' said Eamon quoting the Sermon on the Mount, and we reverted to silence as Eamon took another drag on his cigarette.

Eamon had started blowing smoke rings as a mother and child approached us from the direction of Bruton's.

'Morning, Eamon,' the woman said, a harassed-looking woman with brown hair kept in place by a faded headscarf.

'Morning, Mrs Cassidy,' said Eamon.

'And who's this now?' she said addressing me.

'This is my comrade, Volunteer Mick McAlinden: a man of the Black North, but he's okay.'

'I've heard tell of you, Mick. You're staying with the Bonners.'

'I am,' I said. 'And who is this?' I asked, looking at the frightened-looking child tugging at his mother's skirts.

'This is Stephen. Say hello, Stephen.'

'Hello,' said Stephen in a small voice.

'We've just been in to Bruton's. Poor Stephen has a very sore throat, don't you, son?'

Stephen nodded. 'Doctor said nothing to worry about just keep him home for a day or so and give him tea with honey and lemon.'

'So you got a few days off school, did you? That's not the worst,' I said to Stephen.

He nodded again.

'You're at the National School, are you, Stephen?' I asked.

Stephen nodded again.

'Did you know Liam Finnegan?' Eamon pitched in.

Stephen nodded.

'Aye. Very sad that was,' his mother answered for him. 'Liam was in Stephen's class, wasn't he, Stephen?'

Stephen nodded again.

'And did you see him on Monday at all?'

'No,' said Stephen. 'The master asked if anyone knew where he was when he took the roll, but no one had seen him. The master said he must be off with the snifters or something.'

'That was Master O'Riordain? He said Liam must be off with the snifters or something?'

'Yes,' said Stephen. 'That's what he said.'

'Hmm,' said Eamon.

'It was Monday that Stephen got sick. Such a big boy, you'd think he'd have more sense than being out playing in the rain.'

'The master didn't stop youse?' I asked.

'The master wasn't there!' said Mrs Cassidy. 'So the boys took the notion to play football in the rain while they waited for him. I'd a good mind to speak to him about that, but I know he's carrying quite a burden at the moment, with the battalion as well as the school.'

'How long was the Master away for?' Eamon asked.

'You said he was got back about break time, didn't you, Stephen? I suppose that is about eleven.'

Stephen squeaked something. 'What was that?' asked his mother.

'Yes,' said Stephen, in a small but clear voice.

'And Mrs O'Flaherty' – she was the other teacher at the school – 'she didn't say anything to ye?' asked Eamon.

'Sure that one is only useless, sometimes. I think she has her hands full with the infants.'

'I think you'd better get this young fellow home and some of that honey and lemon into him,' said Eamon.

'I should indeed,' said his mother.

'Nice seeing you, Stephen. Lovely to meet you, Mrs Cassidy,' I said.

'You also, Mick,' she said.

'Give my best to your husband,' said Eamon.

'I will,' she said. 'Come on now, Stephen,' and taking him by the hand she headed down the road.

'Holmes had a thought,' I said once she was out of earshot.

'Enlighten me.'

'"When you have eliminated the impossible, whatever remains, however improbable, must be the truth."'

'You think, however improbable, Crosby was telling the truth?'

'Don't you now?' I asked. 'We never really got to have that close a look at O'Riordain, what with him threatening to shoot us and all. It's like you said, the same old story: power and abuse of power. Them with the power taking what they think is their due and fuck the rest of us. Literally in this case. I can see O'Riordain enticing Liam not just with the prospect of a few bob, but with a prospect for adventure. "Come over to mine. I need a brave dependable lad like yourself, Liam, to undertake some important work for the Republic. But don't tell anyone now. It has to be a secret. The security of the Revolution depends upon it. So don't let anyone see you on your way here either." And O'Riordain's house is big enough and isolated enough to do all sorts in undetected, don't you think?'

'Fuck,' said Eamon.

'What?' I asked.

'We never did chat to those kids at the funeral.'

'We had another line of enquiry.'

'Well, this is a particular one I hoped we would not have to follow.'

'Why not?' I asked.

'Fuck sake, Mick. How much more do you want to fuck up our lives today? Because Peter or no Peter, wandering up to O'Riordain and accusing him of fucking and strangling a child seems to me about the most straightforward way of you and me ending up next to those peelers in the back of the barracks.'

'Are you saying we should just forget about it?'

Eamon looked at me. 'You said that Liam was the youngest dead body you had ever seen.'

'Aye,' I said.

'He was the youngest dead body I have ever seen too.'

'Not something you can easy forget.'

'No. Particularly when you consider that the fucker who did it is still wandering around. My wife would never forgive me if she knew I'd turned my back on this.'

'I thought you said she was dead?'

'The sort of her,' said Eamon, 'that wouldn't fucking stop her.'

XXX

Rather than hanging about outside McLaughlin's office, Eamon proposed we should return to his for breakfast. When we arrived there was a noticeable change in the atmosphere that awaited us. The family were sitting around the kitchen table in silence but they jumped up when we opened the door.

'Where the fuck were you last night?' Brendan asked Eamon.

'We had to go to see Dr Hennessy. She invited us to stay over because of the weather. What's wrong? It's not the first time I have had to stay out on police business.'

'Shamey O'Neill was here looking for you last night.'

'What did he want?' asked Eamon.

'He just said Commandant O'Riordain wanted to see you – IRA business.'

I felt myself breaking out in a cold sweat.

'Was he by himself?' asked Eamon.

'Somebody drove him here in a car. I didn't see who or who else was in the car.'

Eamon was quiet. 'Do you think Peter didn't speak to him yesterday?' I asked.

'Fuck knows,' said Eamon. 'Maybe he wanted us to join the meeting. Maybe he wanted to see us about something completely unrelated. Maybe he just got tired waiting to hear from us and decided to provide some target practice for the lads.'

We started up from the table at the sound of another car approaching. Eamon pulled his Webley out of his belt and cocked it. In that instant, Eamon confirmed that whatever

O'Riordain wanted to talk to us about, Eamon didn't think it was benign. 'Get upstairs, Ma. You too, Fiona. Where's the shotgun, Michael?'

'It's in the forge.'

'Fuck,' said Eamon. ''Twould be best if you went upstairs too then, Brendan.'

I had my own revolver in my hand, but that didn't stop it shaking. The car engine had stopped and we heard footsteps approaching. There was a knock. Eamon levelled his revolver at the door and in a half crouch reached out with his left hand and opened it. Martin Crosby was standing there with a grave look on his face.

'Jesus, Father. You gave us a bit of a fright. We've been a bit on edge this morning.'

'I've been looking for you boys.'

'What for?'

'Peter McLaughlin has been killed.'

We all stood in stunned silence for a moment. I felt my blood pressure drop and for a moment thought I might faint, but instead I managed to find a chair to sit down on and I slowly felt myself return to normal.

'What happened?' Eamon asked.

Crosby related to us what had happened. Perhaps others had passed him by too afraid to say anything, but it was Packy O'Reilly, when he was on his way back from doing Francie Quinn's milking, who raised the alarm. He saw the body lying on the side of the road, hooded and wet through with the night's rain, with a placard tied around its neck: 'Shot as a traitor by the IRA.'

Packy cycled back up to the parochial house and roused Crosby who sent Packy on to get Dr Hennessy. She arrived ten minutes after Crosby who by then had already performed the Last Rites. They loaded the body into the back of Dr Hennessy's car and took it to Toner's. There they removed the hood and found the head barely recognisable as a result of the damage from the gunshots. Nevertheless, from a combination of papers found on the body and certain identifying features which Dr Hennessy recognised, they confirmed Crosby's initial dread: that the corpse was that of Peter McLaughlin.

'Fuck,' said Eamon.

'What do you think happened?' I asked. 'O'Riordain?'

'That would be my first presumption.'

'Do you think he intended something like that for us last night too, if he had found us?' I asked.

'Maybe,' said Eamon. 'Probably. Frankly, I don't fucking know.'

He sat and lit a cigarette. 'What are you thinking?' asked Crosby.

'I'm thinking that Peter was as likely to be a traitor as Pearse or Connolly. So why would Jack have him killed?'

'I can think of a reason,' said Crosby.

'Fuck,' said Eamon.

'What?' I asked.

'I gave Peter that post-mortem report before sending him off to see O'Riordain.'

'So what?' I asked. 'Peter was a careful man. He knew he'd have to step lightly with O'Riordain.'

'But he was also a kind man. You saw how that stuff upset him. You don't think that after he had gone off to brood on it that it might upset him more, upset him enough that he might say something inadvisable? He might have let slip his suspicion. He might have seen something in Jack's reaction to his questions and not have been able to suppress his disgust.'

'Or maybe Jack just had him plugged because he could, or because Peter said something to annoy him, like about him murdering those peelers,' I said.

'Why would he come looking for us then?'

'Perhaps he's thinking that with Peter out of the way he can do what he wants with us. Reinstall us in the battalion, maybe, and then he has us where he wants us – under his authority.'

'Jaysus, Mick. Do you believe any of that oul shite?' Eamon asked.

'No, not really. Just trying to be thorough.'

'That's admirable enough,' said Eamon. 'But I think the greater likelihood is that Jack will indeed still be looking for us now.'

'Indeed,' said Crosby. 'I think you're right, Eamon, and it would probably be a good idea if you boys made yourself scarce for a bit. I can run youse up to Ballina and you can lie low until I find out what is happening. The parish priest there is a friend of mine. I can ask him to put you up.'

Eamon was quiet. I could almost hear the gears grinding as he thought. 'If O'Riordain is accusing parish court officials, starting with Peter, of informing, then us scarpering might be seen as an admission of guilt.'

'But there are more senior court and military officials in Ballina. You can report the matter up to them,' said Crosby.

'We will have the same problem we discussed last night. Evidence. I cannot see anybody wishing to move against such an effective military commandant even with overwhelming evidence, let alone just on our word against his. Even if they don't think that Peter is guilty of informing – and frankly I do not believe that anyone in their right mind would ever believe such unmitigated shite – they are likely to be sympathetic to a commander under pressure who makes a "mistake" and still refuse to move against him. He could be covered in innocent blood up to his armpits and the only thing that would matter to them is has he been killing peelers and Tans as well.'

'What are you suggesting then?'

'Fucked if I know. But I don't want to be bumping into Jack again before we know what we are doing.'

'So?' said Crosby.

'Ballina,' said Eamon. Then he turned to Brendan. 'If Shamey or any of the rest of O'Riordain's lot come around here again, tell them we have gone to Ballina to report Peter's death and ask for further instructions from the registrar of the Republican District Court there.'

'Okay,' said Brendan.

'But don't go looking for him. Indeed, if you can avoid speaking to him at all, do that.'

'Okay,' Brendan repeated.

'Let's be going then, Martin,' Eamon said to Crosby.

'Grand,' said Crosby and he went out through the door.

'Ma,' shouted Eamon up the stairs. 'I'm just off to Ballina with Father Crosby.' Mrs Gleason appeared at the head of the stairs and came back down. 'I should be back in a day or so, so don't be worrying.'

'Take care of yourself, son, will you? You too, Mick,' said Mrs Gleason.

'We will, Ma, now don't be worrying. Sure, after the Kaiser's army tried their best to get rid of me, anyone wants to kill me now would need a silver bullet.'

Eamon gave his mother a kiss on the cheek and then I followed him out the door to Crosby's car.

XXXI

Crosby put us in the back seat of his car, 'Now keep the fuck down, for fuck sake.'

'You know, Martin,' said Eamon as we sat bent over with our heads behind the front seats, 'I've been around a few military padres but your language really does take the biscuit.'

'My superiors have been telling me that since the seminary. But I'm forty now, so I've given up on trying to change it.'

'You can take the boy out of the bog, but you can't take the bog out of the boy.'

'Aye,' said Crosby. 'Something like that. Except it was a tenement.'

Eamon smiled. 'Thanks for coming looking for us, by the way. 'Twas very good of you to keep an eye out for us. Particularly given some of the things we have been saying about you these past days.'

'You can thank Sophia as well for that. For some reason she seems to like you.'

'Hmm,' said Eamon.

We were out of town now and I was beginning to breathe easier. We both sat up in the back seat of the car. I leaned forward to look out the windscreen but Eamon reclined back, still ruminating.

'If O'Riordain, as seems likely, had Peter plugged, because of allegations that Peter made regarding the death of Liam,' he said, 'it seems unlikely that the whole battalion was involved. It's more likely just a few like Shamey, who Jack can get to do his bidding. With buffoons like Shamey about it wouldn't matter if Peter had St Patrick there vouching for him, Shamey would take no notice, and just say yes Jack, no Jack, three bags full Jack. Jack would not risk the whole battalion being involved in something as vile and potentially divisive as murdering Peter just in case one of the fuckers spontaneously grew a conscience and a pair of balls.'

'Jack seemed able enough to get the whole battalion to do his bidding when he had them killing them cops,' said Martin.

'That was different. It was after a firefight when we had lost some of our own, and nobody liked that bastard Finucane anyway.'

'The station sergeant?'

'The very one. I think even his mother had difficulty loving that ugly Limerick fucker.'

'Maybe,' said Martin. 'But the rest of them in that barracks were okay. That young constable, Harris, he was a lovely young man, expecting his first child.'

'I've heard others say that too.'

Eamon was silent for a while. 'Intelligence matters tend to be conducted on a need-to-know basis. And even if this was a legitimate enquiry into a suspected informer it would have been a big ask to get the whole battalion to line up against somebody like Peter. I mean, I don't know anyone with a bad word to say about him, or who he had a bad word to say about… Apart from you, that is.'

'We had a bit of a falling out over the Dáil courts. It was bad timing, really. He came to see me about it shortly after O'Riordain conducted his little massacre at the barracks. I was a bit blunt with him. But I always respected him.'

'Hmm,' said Eamon. 'I'm paraphrasing a bit here but I think he said something along the lines of, "I never liked that fucker Crosby." That is a rather absolute position for a daily communicant to take of his priest and confessor.'

'I can't imagine Peter using language like that.'

'Maybe it was just a "fecker" he thought you were, so.'

'When was this?'

'Thursday afternoon.'

'Hmm,' said Martin. 'I wonder did he suspect about me and Sophia.'

'Why would he?'

'Well, he called up to the house one day shortly after our affair started, with some paperwork related to her husband's will. I happened to be there. You know what it is like, new lovers. He might have picked up on something.'

'Jaysus,' said Eamon. 'Sophia said you were good to her after her husband died. I honestly didn't realise just how good.'

'Cheeky bastard,' said Martin, and we drove along in silence for a while.

'This is a pointless excursion,' said Eamon.

'Why?' asked Martin.

'Pull in up there,' said Eamon pointing to a side road leading up into a stand of trees. Martin complied.

'O'Riordain is a cute hoor. The only reason he can have killed Peter is if he perceived him as a threat. I don't know if he thinks the threat is neutralised now, but it seems unlikely and chances are if he perceived Peter as a threat he will perceive us as a threat too, just to tie up the loose ends. Now he might, just, spare us if we go to him right now and say we had no idea of what Peter was up to. But I doubt it. And, you know, an ex-British Army NCO and a blow-in from the north, there will be a lot in these parts just automatically regard us with suspicion and without knowing the facts will presume we got what was coming to us. Even with knowing the facts they would still presume, just out of gobshite, small town, inbred principle, that we got what was coming to us anyway if we ended up in a bog somewhere.

'But even if we could get on the right side of O'Riordain,' Eamon continued, 'that would bring no justice for Liam and no protection for any other kids in these parts. And continuing on to Ballina to throw ourselves on the mercy of the Brigade and more senior Dáil officials there is not likely to bring any justice to either Peter or Liam. Jack will have better contacts there than we have or Peter had, and the word of a living hero of the Republic will carry greater weight than that of a dead, alleged traitor.'

'So what are you suggesting?' asked Martin.

'If we have dirty linen to wash, I think it's the sort of thing we should clean up in Ballykennedy, don't you?'

'So how do we do that? O'Riordain is still cock of the walk with thirty armed men behind him.'

'Try not to worry, fellas. You know what Peter Pan said, "anything is possible if only you wish hard enough".'

XXXII

When we turned back on the road from Ballina, Eamon told Crosby to take us to Francie Quinn's house. Mrs Quinn showed the three of us into the front room where Francie was again sitting at his desk, but this time he was staring blankly out of the window.

'What do you boys want this time?' he asked.

'I suppose we are after a court ruling,' Eamon said.

'What about?'

'Peter.'

'Haven't you heard? O'Riordain has taken that matter out of our hands.'

'You have heard?'

'O'Riordain came to see me this morning to apprise me of the situation.'

'Why you?'

'Because of my roles on the parish court, and my recent appointment as his adjutant.'

This was news to me, and I felt a spasm of panic in my gut. I wondered if we had walked into a trap about to be sprung by O'Riordain's new second in command. Involuntarily, my hand twitched towards the butt of my revolver. But as Eamon still appeared composed I suppressed the instinct. When he had told Martin to drive us here, he said, 'Peter always told me that I could trust Francie, and said that if he was ever not about that I shouldn't hesitate to speak to him. So, all in all, that seems to me to be our best gambit at this point in the game.'

I reflected as we drove that in chess the gambit involved the sacrifice of a piece, usually a pawn, for the sake of positional advantage, and the last time I had tried such a stratagem against Eamon I ended up being slaughtered.

'When were you appointed adjutant?' he asked Francie.

'At the start of the week.'

'Is that what he was speaking to you about on Monday?'

'Yes. He had asked me some time ago to become quartermaster but I refused.'

'Why?'

'Because I did not want to be under the authority of ignorant, fucking gobshites like Shamey O'Neill.'

'But finally he agreed to appoint you adjutant to get over that particular problem.'

'He did. He has an acute supply problem which he knows I can help him fix given that I am still trading livestock across much of the west of Ireland, something that he and I agreed would make a decent cover for the transport of arms and ammunition.'

Something seemed to have loosened up in Quinn since we spoke to him on Thursday morning. He was displaying none of the arrogance or defensiveness he showed then, even when we were asking him about military matters. I presumed that the shock of Peter's death had shaken him quite profoundly and his need to talk to anyone, even us, was overwhelming.

'Well, then, if you are Jack's adjutant, then shouldn't you have been involved in Peter's court martial?'

'You would suppose that. It is the very question I asked Jack this morning when he came to tell me about it.'

'What did he say?'

'He said that given my role on the parish court, and my friendship with Peter, he felt I might have a conflict of interest.'

'That's what he said? "A conflict of interest"?'

'Yes.'

'That man has been a cunt since first I knew him and is a murderous cunt now.'

Francie was quiet for a while. 'He's certainly a hard man. Naively, I did not anticipate my involvement in military affairs would implicate me so closely in the death of a friend.'

'So how did he justify what he had done to Peter?'

'He said some disturbing facts had come to light that caused him to suspect Peter was gathering intelligence for the British. He confronted Peter with the accusation and Peter confessed everything. He convened a hastily gathered court martial and passed sentence.'

'So you think Peter was a traitor too?'

'I do in my fuck,' said Quinn. 'There was as much chance of Peter being a traitor as me being a traitor and I know there is no chance of that.'

'Did Jack mention us?'

'Why would he?'

'Shamey O'Neill was at mine last night. We don't know if he had gone to the Bonners to look for Mick. Both of us were abroad, so we don't know what Jack had in mind for us.'

'Why would he have anything in mind for you?'

We summarised for Francie our enquiry into the death of Liam from the confirmation of Eamon's initial suspicions up to our conversation with O'Riordain.

'So I was a suspect in Liam's death too?'

'You have a car.'

'And that, presumably, is why Peter never mentioned your nosing around to me before you came to visit?'

'We didn't think there was a need. You accounted for your whereabouts convincingly.'

'But he came to see me on Thursday night.'

'We worried that you might mention to Jack that we had been asking you about sensitive military matters, and Jack might decide that was evidence enough to have us shot.'

'Why would he do such a thing?'

'Well, he never liked us much to begin with and he did intimate that the shooting of us had crossed his mind.'

'When?'

'When we asked him about his use of his car on Monday morning.'

'You think that was a sore point with him?'

'It certainly seems that way.'

'Well, if he was on to you, why didn't he just have you plugged straight away?'

'When we spoke to Jack we said that we were enquiring into Liam's death to try to prevent future such tragic accidents. We did not tell him that we had a medical report that proved that Liam had not only been murdered but that he had been sexually assaulted before his death.'

'Sexually assaulted? How?'

'There was evidence from the medical examination that his hands had been bound and he had been gagged. He was also anally raped.'

'Jesus fucking Christ,' said Francie.

'Indeed,' said Eamon. 'I think that Peter let slip to Jack that we knew Liam had been murdered. I had given him the medical report before he went to see Jack. He might have brooded on it and said something in anger that let Jack know we were on to him. Or perhaps Peter saw something in Jack and knew he was a child-killer. Whatever happened, Jack used his extraordinary powers as an IRA commander in wartime to cover up the fact of Liam's murder by framing for treason and executing the most important official in the parish who was aware that a crime had been committed.'

'As a theory, this hinges on the supposition that O'Riordain did indeed murder Liam.'

'We have some additional evidence that corroborates the theory that Jack was responsible for Liam's death.'

'Like what?'

'He was late for school the morning of Liam's death. Very late – he arrived around break time. When we spoke to him he said it was a normal morning. He had concluded some reports at home and got to school nine-ish. So he had opportunity.'

'That is a flimsy basis to presume a man guilty of murder. He could simply have lost track of time. If that is all you had, Jack would not have been spooked. He'd have died laughing.'

We looked at each other. 'There are some other matters which we are not at liberty to disclose,' said Eamon.

'I would suggest you disclose them. Frankly, what this looks like is you are seeking to undermine an officer of the Irish Republic, and that does come somewhere close to treason in my book.'

Crosby had been silent all this time. Finally he spoke. 'The evidence that they are referring to is from me. On the same day that Liam died, O'Riordain tried to make his confession to me. He told me in some considerable detail how he had killed Liam.'

Francie looked at Martin. 'Hold on. Are you telling me that O'Riordain admitted to you in confession that he had murdered Liam?'

'Yes.'

'So you have just broken the seal of confession. Doesn't that bring with it automatic excommunication?'

'I did not think that O'Riordain was properly disposed towards the sacrament.'

'So you can just decide that for yourself now, can you?'

'Perhaps you can permit me and my superiors to be concerned about my moral failings and possible infractions of canon law and instead focus on your responsibilities in the civil sphere.'

'Which are?'

'Which are how do you ensure that no other children of this parish befall the sort of dreadful fate that came to Liam Finnegan?'

Francie said nothing. I decided to speak. 'One of the last times we spoke to Peter he said it's not killing and "blood sacrifice" that makes a nation. It's taking care of each other and protecting the weak that does. He believed that the role of the Dáil courts was to show the world that we can run our own affairs, and fundamental to the nation we want to be is the principle that no one is above the law.'

'I'm not a lawyer. Peter generally guided us on such matters in the parish court. But it seems to me that there is not enough to convict on the evidence you have presented,' said Francie. 'What is the phrase they use in the criminal cases? "Beyond reasonable doubt".'

Eamon spoke again, 'I am convinced that Jack raped and killed Liam. I know he murdered those peelers at the barracks. And I know he murdered Peter. He told you as much and you know that he lied about his reason, even if you are unsure about what his motivation actually was.'

Eamon leaned back in his chair and folded his arms. 'I believe O'Riordain killed Peter because Peter knew Liam was murdered and O'Riordain was fearful that Peter might find out that he was responsible. What sort of country are we going to find ourselves in if we let this fucker, or fuckers like him, continue unchecked? We could find that we have thrown out one oppressor to replace them with another, one with the same scant regard for the welfare of the children of this or any other parish, or the welfare of anyone who is weaker than them. One who decides that power alone is the arbiter of what can be gotten away with and to hell with them that are weak. I don't know about you, Francie, but the last thing I want to do is to see the oppression of the British Empire replicated in this country once the British have gone.'

Francie looked at Eamon. 'I feel we are at an abyss no matter which way we turn.'

'Aye,' said Eamon. 'It is called war.'

XXXIII

It was early evening and we were back in Sophia's house, sitting in the kitchen drinking tea. Crosby and Sophia had gone off, ostensibly to look for a change of clothes for us elsewhere in the house.

'Do you think they are fucking now?' Eamon asked suddenly.

'Jesus sake, Eamon. Do you think of nothing else?'

'Occasionally I think of social justice. Sometimes I reminisce on the war. From time to time I contemplate the great works of literature. But most of the time I like to think about naked women. It's like my hobby.'

'How long were you married?' I asked.

'I met her at the beginning of 1915. We got married in January 1918, and she was killed in August.'

'Did you meet her in hospital?'

'No, I met her in a café in Paris when I was convalescing. Got to tell you, Mick, the most useful subject I ever studied at the Christian Brothers was French.'

I smiled at that. 'I never had much of a facility for languages,' I said.

'Well, you are a young man yet. Keep it up. One day we will be sitting together drinking fine wine on the Champs-Élysées. I don't want to have to do all the work for you when the mademoiselles show up.'

'Sure what would they see in a bogman like me?'

'In Ireland, Mick, you're a bogman, and you'll always be a bogman no matter how many degrees you end up with. In France you are a sophisticated stranger.'

'Really?'

'Really … At least if you can speak a bit of French, don't smell and finally manage to read *War and Peace*.'

'So you charmed your wife with your knowledge of Russian literature?'

'Aye. It's a weakness them French communists have these days.'

'Was it love at first sight?'

'Well, it was fancy at first sight, and when a Frenchwoman says "Oh la la" it does have the power to melt the heart of even the stoniest of bastards. I suppose I knew it was love when I realised that I wanted her to have my army pension if I bought it. Strangely, she did not find that the most romantic of proposals. But I think I must have made it up to her eventually because she said yes. I never in a thousand years would have thought it would be me end up collecting her pension instead.'

We drank our tea.

'How do they feel about Shakespeare, the French?' I asked.

'What? You don't have any stomach for a new literature?'

'Not so much that, but you do seem to have a considerable knowledge of the Bard. I was wondering if that had aided your romantic endeavours.'

'Ach, I've read a few of his plays, and seen a few more in London and Dublin. But I'd hardly be an expert.'

'Is *Hamlet* your favourite?'

'Why do you ask?'

'Well, you knew about the "country matters" pun.'

'I wouldn't say it was my favourite. I've read it a few times. It always pleases me when the little fucker gets knifed at the end.'

'Why so?'

'Because that play is a cautionary tale for the likes of us.'

'Princes of Denmark?'

He laughed. 'No. Revolutionaries. Think of it. Hamlet, and there's another needy little spoiled prick if ever there was one, never a good word to say about anyone. Decides to organise a coup d'état and put his own arse on the throne instead of his uncle. Fucks it up completely. Murders poor Polonius, and drives his daughter to suicide, and all Ophelia ever did was like the little bastard. But that doesn't stop him. Off he goes with a trail of carnage behind him. First time I read it I was hoping Laertes would plug the little bastard because it's what the fucker deserved and no better man to do it than one whose life and happiness have been destroyed by the incompetent little fucker. I'll tell you if you are going to plot revolution with all the mayhem, bloodshed and chaos that entails then you'd better do it effectively or else you deserve every fucking thing you get.'

'If you have to kill something, don't fuck about?'

'Exactly!'

'You know you might have something there, Eamon. You must get sick of being right all the time.'

'Ach, it's something I could live with, I think. But you know, Mick, I've been thinking about something that I got wrong.'

'What was that?'

'I said, in war you should just do your job.'

'I remember.'

'Juliette was just doing her job and she still got killed. She had been over three years in the army. She would never have taken an unnecessary risk. We talked about it. She was always careful. Peter was just doing his job and got killed. Maybe if Peter had been a bit more careful he might not have died, but I'm not so sure about that given the sort of cunt O'Riordain is. They both got killed doing jobs that they took upon themselves because they were kind people. Just like those stretcher-bearers who saved my life. Just like that young English fella Vic Brotherton who got plugged trying to help me. Juliette and Peter were two of the best people I've ever known. The world is a bleaker place without them or Corporal Brotherton. Perhaps young Liam would have been one of them had he lived, part of that fraternity of decency that tries to be nice and caring even when the world is going to shite.'

'So what's the moral of the story?'

'Maybe what you said the first time: be kind, be careful, and hope for the best because you can never know what shite fate has in store for you anyway. Otherwise we just end up as cunts like Jack, or the Black and Tans, or heaven forfend, Shamey O-fucking-Neill. And what a bleak shite hole of the world those fuckers would make for us if they had their way. At the end of the day it is perhaps not love, or courage, or even wisdom that are the greatest virtues. It's kindness that is the foundation of all the others.'

'I am not sure that anyone would ever suggest that I was possessed of any of those virtues.'

'Maybe not, Mick,' Eamon said. 'Maybe not now. But I believe you are the sort of man who is prepared to do the right thing, irrespective of the cost. And that is also a virtue, albeit a fucking thankless one.'

We were quiet for a while more and then Eamon spoke again.

'Look,' he said, 'I would not be suggesting this if it was just about saving our own skins. I believe it is the right thing to do.'

'I know,' I said.

XXXIV

We waited until nine o'clock before we moved. We went out the back door of Sophia's house and moved far out into the fields before we started hiking towards O'Riordain's.

'Do you think it's going to rain?' I asked. We heard a peal of distant thunder as we crossed another ditch.

'Mick, it's always going to rain. It's Ireland!'

The route Eamon picked would only have taken us about an hour in daylight. But in darkness it took us twice that time. Finally, we came to what Eamon called our rally point on a hillside about a quarter of a mile above O'Riordain's house. We took position behind a dry-stone wall and Eamon pulled a pair of field glasses out of the haversack that Crosby had recovered for him from his brother, Brendan, earlier in the day.

Eamon scanned the darkness.

'What are you looking for?' I asked. Aside from a light in O'Riordain's kitchen the darkness was almost absolute. I had no idea which phase of the moon it was but even if it had been full it would have made no difference through so overcast a sky.

'Cigarettes,' Eamon said. I remembered how Eamon had told me of a young man, new to the trenches, who he had seen shot through the mouth one night by a sniper. The kid had been trying to calm his nerves by smoking, but a German had zeroed in on the glow of the ash. 'Lucky for the young fellow the wound was fatal,' Eamon had said and I shuddered at the thought of the disfigurement the bullet must have inflicted to obtain that verdict.

'You think they will be stupid enough to be smoking if they are on sentry duty?'

'I'm doubtful enough that there is anyone on sentry duty. There hasn't been before now. But if there is, I am pretty confident that they would be dumb enough to smoke. O'Riordain is a bit of a martinet about some things, but I never found him to be that sharp on field craft or drill.'

'He was competent enough to take the barracks.'

'Aye, and he lost three doing that. If they had been more soundly disciplined they may have learned some basic lessons about not exposing themselves in the middle of a firefight.'

Eamon continued to scan the darkness for about another twenty minutes. I took a bottle of water out of my knapsack, took a long swallow, and then offered it to Eamon.

'Thanks,' he said, and took a swig.

'Okay,' said Eamon. 'I don't think there is anyone there. Let's move down to the boundary wall for a closer look.' It took us about twenty minutes to descend from our rally point to the wall behind O'Riordain's house.

It was just past midnight when a light came on in another window, I presume the bedroom. The light went off after about ten minutes.

'Shite,' said Eamon.

'What is it?'

'Well, either he has gone to sleep and habitually left the light on in the kitchen, or he has gone back into the kitchen.'

'So what do we do?'

'Wait,' said Eamon.

After a few minutes the back door of the house opened and O'Riordain came out. Illuminated in the light from his kitchen we could see him, empty-handed and in his shirtsleeves, walk to the outside toilet and go inside.

'We're in luck,' Eamon whispered and clapped me on the shoulder.

Our original plan was to wait until O'Riordain was asleep and then break into the house to arrest him in his bedclothes. We had discussed waiting until early in the morning when he would be going through his deepest phase of sleep and hence most disorientated. But neither of us liked the idea of confronting him with that Mauser in his own house.

Nevertheless, it was the best plan either of us could come up with. But Eamon had said, 'it's like chess', and we might deviate from the plan if a suitable opportunity arose. His midnight piss was such an opportunity.

We sprinted as quietly as we could in our boots, towards the outhouse and took position on either side of the door. I tried to control my breathing but was already breathing heavily.

'Who's there?' Jack shouted from inside the toilet.

Eamon didn't answer. Instead he suddenly moved from in front of the door and swung his boot with full force at the latch. It splintered and the whole door caved. I heard

O'Riordain grunt as the door hit him. Eamon was already launching himself at the door again. This time he hit the thing with both feet. He took it off its hinges and I heard O'Riordain grunt again.

Eamon got up off the ground. He pulled the Webley from his belt and a torch from another pocket. He lit up the doorway with the torch. 'Get the door, Mick,' he shouted.

I pulled the door away to reveal O'Riordain bloody and dazed, still on the toilet with his trousers around his ankles. O'Riordain raised his hand to shield himself from the glare. 'Cover him,' Eamon said. I took my own Webley out of my belt, gripped it with both hands, and pointed it at O'Riordain. Eamon pushed his revolver back into his belt and moved forward to grab O'Riordain by the front of his shirt and pull him out of the toilet and into the yard. Then he kicked the feet from under O'Riordain who went down hard on his knees. Eamon stepped behind him then and, using the torch, which he had switched to his right hand, struck him with a powerful blow across the back of the neck. O'Riordain went down face first onto the ground.

I swear to this day that Eamon had already got his haversack off his back before O'Riordain hit the ground. He pulled out a length of rope and quickly bound O'Riordain's hands behind his back. 'Lift his head,' he said to me. I did and Eamon stuffed a rag into the prone man's mouth which he secured with another, shorter length of rope. Finally he pulled an empty flour sack from Sophia's kitchen out of his bag and hooded O'Riordain.

'Okay, Mick. Time to move.'

We each reached under one of his armpits and dragged him round to the side of his house. His trousers and underpants were still around his ankles.

Eamon pointed his torch up the street and signalled – three long flashes. In the distance a car engine started and moved towards us. 'Thank Jesus for that,' Eamon said. I knew he had a backup signal of a whistle blast, but neither of us had wanted to attract that much attention.

The car turned into O'Riordain's gate and pulled up in front of the house. The driver cut the engine and Martin Crosby got out.

'Thanks, Martin. We'll take this from here.'

'What are you going to do with him?' Martin asked.

'Nothing for you to worry about. It is a matter for the courts now.'

We loaded him into the back of the car and I sat with a gun at his head. 'Shouldn't we pull up his trousers?' I asked.

'No. We want him compliant and a man with his balls exposed to the world tends to be rather more docile,' said Eamon. Then he turned to Crosby. 'We'll see you tomorrow, Martin.'

'Aye, God willing.'

SUNDAY

XXXV

WE DROVE A narrow back road out of town up further into the hills. After half an hour Eamon slowed the car and pulled in off the road beside another car.

'Stay here a minute, will you,' he said to me and he got out. In the light of the headlights I saw him walking up to meet another man: Francie Quinn, who was leaning against the hood of his car.

After a few moments Eamon came back. 'Okay,' he said. 'The place is ready.'

O'Riordain had come to about ten minutes before, but the combination of my revolver against his head and the night air against his balls had kept him quiet. But Eamon's words caused him to piss himself all over me and the back seat of Crosby's car.

'Fuck sake,' I said and jumped out of the door.

I looked at Eamon, half expecting him to make some sort of a joke, but he was grim-faced. He opened the back door of the car, took O'Riordain by the collar of his shirt and pulled him out of the car.

'Help me get his trousers up, Mick. We have a bit of walking to do.' Between the two of us we pulled them back up and belted them into position. Then he took O'Riordain by the elbow and twisted him away from the road. 'Keep him covered now, Mick. Move it, Jack.'

We left Francie at the cars with his shotgun broken across his arm and Eamon's field glasses to keep lookout. Then we walked with O'Riordain for about fifty yards, until we got behind a small hillock that shielded us from the road. Eamon pulled the hood from his head and undid the bow knot he had used to tie the gag in place. The rope fell away and Eamon snapped the rag out of O'Riordain's mouth.

'I think you know why you are here, Jack,' said Eamon.

'You have no right,' said Jack.

'I'm afraid the idea of rights and protections took a bit of a hit in these parts since you murdered Peter.'

'I did not murder Peter. I have a responsibility to maintain the security of the military operations we are waging in these parts. McLaughlin was a threat to that. I have a responsibility to the men under my command.'

'I suppose we could discuss that all night but we don't really have time for that. Let me sum this up. In the extraordinary circumstances in which we find ourselves, the parish court of Ballykennedy has reviewed the evidence against you and agreed that to protect the lives and safety of the citizens of this parish, in time of war, to pass a death sentence upon you. It will be carried out forthwith. Now, do you have anything you wish to say?'

'What sort of fucking shite is this?' said O'Riordain. 'You hold some sort of kangaroo court without even giving me a chance to defend myself?'

'It's tough, I know,' said Eamon, 'but there is a war on.'

'Peter McLaughlin had the chance to defend himself.'

'Fat lot of good that did him.'

'There was compelling evidence against him.'

'Like what?'

'Shamey saw him last week at the Balinrobe races, consorting with the enemy.'

'Consorting how? Standing in the general proximity of some British officers?'

'Drinking with them.'

'Peter didn't drink.'

'Well, he was acting very friendly anyway. Then you two gobshites sticking your nose into matters that did not concern you at Peter's behest confirmed he was up to something traitorous.'

'Horseshite,' said Eamon.

'What? You think all those trips to the races he used to go on were innocent? It's how he met his British contacts, army friends of his son.'

'That's fucking horseshite, and you're a lying bastard.'

'No, it's true. I swear it.'

'Why would Peter betray his country to the very empire that caused the death of his son?'

'For money. Why else do you think? The paid informer has been the curse of every Irish independence movement through history. Today is no different. Them horses are an expensive habit and the British knew their man.'

'So it is a complete coincidence that Peter picked the night that you had decided to court martial him to go and interview you about Liam Finnegan?'

'What the fuck is this about Liam Finnegan? Peter never mentioned him. We lifted him from his office after that girl who works for him had gone home. We went looking for you two at the same time but you'd made yourselves scarce.'

'Lucky for us.'

'Not so lucky for the Republic,' said Jack.

'This has nothing to do with the Republic, Jack,' said Eamon. 'This is about Liam Finnegan.'

'What the fuck are ye talking about?'

'Crosby told us.'

'Crosby told you what?'

'Crosby told us you had confessed about killing Liam to him.'

'Liam Finnegan drowned in an accident.'

'Somebody wanted everyone to believe Liam drowned. He didn't. He was strangled after having been raped.'

'And Crosby told you I confessed that to him, did he?'

'He did, aye.'

'Sure that West British bastard would say anything to blacken the name of any member of the IRA, let alone a commandant. Did you ever think of that?'

'We did, aye. But then Peter wound up dead when he went to speak to you about Liam, and we discovered you were absent from school the morning Liam was killed, giving you plenty of time to fuck and kill the child.'

'This is all fucking lies. Peter never mentioned Liam Finnegan to me. He was busy enough that evening denying his own treachery.'

'Well, we could stand here all night, Jack, and listen to your tall tales about Peter, but that is not why we came here, is it?'

'McLaughlin picked ye two fuckers well. Cut from the same cloth. Ye two fuckers are doing the work of the British. Traitors. Ye are nothing but fucking traitors.'

'I don't believe a word you are saying about Peter, Jack. But if I did, what do you expect us to do? Let you go? I'm sure you would be all sweet reasonableness after that, wouldn't you?'

Jack said nothing.

'Fair play to you, Jack, for not lying,' said Eamon. 'No, our lives would be forfeit if we were to let you go now. You'd turn Shamey O'Neill and your dogs upon us. So you see there really is only one way this night is going to end, isn't there?'

Jack was quiet for a moment and then: 'I need a priest. You can't do this to me without letting me make my confession.'

'Now, now,' said Eamon. 'You know as well as we do that under the circumstances an Act of Contrition, sincerely meant, is as good as confession and absolution.'

'Not for me,' he said, 'not with some of the things that I've done.'

'Aye,' said Eamon. 'We know some of the things that you have done. That's why you're here. But I'm afraid an Act of Contrition is the best we can do for you. And I think if we are prepared to take that risk, you should be too.'

He let out a whelp of anguish at that, and the tears started to stream down his face.

Eamon was unmoved. 'I imagine Liam Finnegan would have begged for his life if he had been able to get a word out as you choked him. I know those cops you had the boys kill certainly did. What did Peter McLaughlin say to you before you falsely accused him of treason and murdered him? So less of your fucking self-pity, O'Riordain.'

I'm not sure if O'Riordain heard him because he was already bent over gagging.

'For fuck sake, Jack,' said Eamon after O'Riordain straightened back up on his knees. 'I'll tell you what. I'll help you out here. Now pay attention: "O my God, I am heartily sorry for having offended Thee, and I detest all my sins because of Thy just punishments, but most of all because they offend Thee, my God, Who art all-good and deserving of all my love. I firmly resolve, with the help of Thy grace, to sin no more and to avoid the near occasions of sin."'

O'Riordain said nothing. 'Look on the bright side, Jack,' said Eamon. 'There'll definitely be no more near occasions of sin for you.' At that O'Riordain bent over and vomited again.

'Okay Mick,' Eamon said. 'No more fucking about. Let's get this show on the road.'

XXXVI

That Saturday afternoon, before we went any further with our deliberations and hours before we were to come across O'Riordain in an outhouse, Eamon had turned to Martin and asked him if he could do him a favour.

'What is it?' asked Martin.

'Could you run back to my place, please, and ask my brother Brendan to get you my old army kit bag. It's in a trunk at the foot of my bed. There's some gear in it that I might be needing.'

Martin complied and we listened as the engine of his car faded. Then the three of us went back to contemplating the abyss.

Eamon, Francie and myself had agreed that if we reported Jack's excesses any further up the chain of command there would be no action taken. He would shake off Peter's murder with some cooked-up record of a court martial with, no doubt, sworn statements from Shamey O'Neill or some other gobshite that Peter had admitted his guilt before he was shot. As for Liam, we could express our suspicions but without witnesses there was no way we could get a conviction, and Crosby would be useless as a witness. It looked like Jack was set to enjoy increasing power in the chaos of the coming months and Christ alone knew what sick shite he might get up to.

However, Francie, finally, as acting chair of the parish court, had decided that given what we knew about Peter, he was prepared under the circumstances, to exceed his authority and pass sentence. This he duly did. 'Death.'

I raised a faint and almost half-hearted protest. 'Is there no other way?'

'Jaysus, Mick. It's not like sending him to Broadmoor hospital for the criminally fucked up is an option here.'

I had no answer to that.

'So, Eamon,' said Francie. 'How do we make this happen?'

In spite of the façade of legality we had endeavoured to achieve and his conviction that the sentence was just, Eamon was pragmatic.

'It would be better if no one knew what became of Jack,' he said.

'What are you suggesting?' Francie asked.

'Well, if we walk up to his front door and shoot him, folk will immediately presume that it was some sort of local feud, and as friends of Peter, a considerable measure of suspicion may fall upon us. However, if the British wanted him dead they would lift him in order to interrogate him first. See if they could gather any useful intelligence on operations in these parts.' Hence we had hatched the plan to arrest him.

Afterwards, sitting at Sophia's kitchen table and talking through the details with Eamon as we checked our weapons and the equipment Martin had retrieved for us I asked, 'Isn't there another way?'

'Fucked if I can think of one,' said Eamon.

'Doesn't it bother you, the thought of killing another human being?'

'It does,' said Eamon. 'But necessity starkly clarifies some choices. We can't lock him up. And if we tried to banish him he would just tell us to fuck off, that is, of course, if he didn't just decide to plug us and be done with it. And suppose he did agree to be banished, what's to stop him torturing other children to death in another parish, or another county, or another country?'

Eamon finished loading the revolver he had just cleaned and snapped shut the magazine. 'Anyway,' he said, 'I'm not going to be the one doing the killing.'

'Who is then?'

'You,' said Eamon.

I suddenly felt faint and sat down before my legs gave out beneath me.

'It's like this,' said Eamon. 'The British may be out of this area for now. But they won't be for ever. As soon as the weather permits, there will be a counter-offensive. That means there is going to be a lot more fighting. Now I've seen it before, in France, youngsters at their first taste of battle hesitate at the moment of truth. It gets you killed. I don't want that happening to you, Mick. This is an opportunity to inoculate yourself, if you will, against the revulsion of killing.'

'I've heard that line before. From O'Riordain. It's how he justified killing those cops.'

'Even a stopped cunt is right twice a day,' Eamon said.

There was a packet of cigarettes sitting on the table between us. 'Give me one of them things, will you?' I said.

Eamon proffered me the packet. I drew one out and placed it between my lips. Eamon lit it for me and I drew a long pull of smoke into my lungs. That set me coughing, but I could feel the tobacco calming me. I took another puff and this time I didn't cough.

'I am not sure I want to inoculate myself against the revulsion of killing people,' I said.

'Good. You shouldn't. But this is war. You do not have the luxury of peacetime.'

SUNDAY

XXXVII

I was already soaked through with sweat. In Sophia's kitchen, the whole thing seemed abstract. Now with the man's piss covering my trousers it was altogether more concrete.

I fumbled with the hammer of my Webley. I was shaking. 'Steady now, Mick,' said Eamon.

I passed the revolver from my right to left hand and wiped the sweat from my palm on the leg of my trouser. Then I switched it back to my right hand and wiped my left hand. I took a deep breath then and tried to steady myself. I knew that the hammer of the Webley rested on an empty chamber to prevent any accidents. As I cocked the revolver the magazine twisted and brought a round into position, ready for firing.

'Now, Jack,' said Eamon, 'a final word of advice. It would be best if you were still now or else this is going to be a lot harder on you than it needs to be.'

O'Riordain blinked the tears out of his eyes and seemed to relax for a second. Then with an extraordinary suddenness he launched himself head first at Eamon. It was a forlorn effort. Eamon sidestepped him and managed to trip him as he passed. O'Riordain fell heavily, crunching into the ground, unable to check his fall with his hands tied behind his back.

Even with this sudden start Eamon seemed the model of composure, at least relative to me. I was relieved to find that I had neither dropped nor accidentally discharged the Webley in the commotion.

'Do it now, Mick,' said Eamon, 'and be quick about it. This is only going to get worse for the bastard if you don't.'

I took a deep breath and walked towards the prone heap of O'Riordain, illuminated in the light of Eamon's torch, lying face down in the grass. He groaned.

I remembered what Eamon had told me about firing the Webley and braced my right wrist with my left hand. The revolver was at the apex of the triangle I made with my arms. I pointed the barrel at the base of his skull. I was only about three feet from him and I could smell the piss and vomit off him. I am not sure, but I think I heard him whimper in the moment before I fired.

The kick startled me so much as I pressed the trigger that I barely registered the report. Blood and something else – perhaps O'Riordain's skull or brains – arced in the torchlight. I was aware of O'Riordain's body spasming as the bullet hit him.

I cocked the revolver again and brought it back to bear on O'Riordain's prone form. I fired a second time, again following Eamon's advice. 'Two normally is enough.'

As the echoes died away I became aware of Eamon standing beside me.

'Check your weapon, Mick,' he said.

My eyes refocused on the Webley.

'Just make it safe for now,' said Eamon. I returned the hammer to rest on a chamber containing one of the expended cartridges and stuffed the revolver into one of my jacket pockets.

My mouth was dry, but I managed to croak, 'Is he dead?'

Eamon leaned forward and played his flashlight across the body of O'Riordain to illuminate his mutilated head and a gaping wound between his shoulder blades. 'I'd say so,' said Eamon. 'He certainly smells it.' The acrid smell of shite came from O'Riordain's corpse.

Now it was my turn to throw up. Even though I had eaten nothing since we had agreed to kill O'Riordain, my body still seemed to find plenty to eject.

Eamon left me to it, but when I had straightened back up he was standing close to me again with a British Army issue water flask that he had retrieved from his haversack. 'Here,' he said.

I washed my mouth out and then took a long drink. I emptied the bottle and handed it back to Eamon. He put it into his pack and then dug his hand in his jacket pocket and pulled out a packet of cigarettes. He offered them to me. I took one, my hands still shaking, and he did the same. He replaced the cigarette packet in his pocket and retrieved his lighter. He offered me the flame first and then lit his own. I sucked the smoke deep into my lungs and felt it calming me.

We smoked in silence for a few minutes. Then Eamon said, 'Right. Let's get this fucker buried.'

We took a foot each – I certainly didn't want to risk touching O'Riordain's blood or brain matter – and dragged him over to the hole Francie had dug. We walked either side of the grave until what was left of his head fell into the hole. Then we dropped his feet in after him. He lay in a crumpled heap in the bottom and I could not help feeling a pang of sorrow and shame that such a fearsome figure had been reduced to this.

Francie had left the shovel. We took turns filling the dirt on top of him. I was struck that the normal hollow echoing of earth and stone onto a coffin was missing. Instead the sound of the gravel falling on the corpse sounded more like rain.

Eamon had the last turn with the shovel to finish the burial. 'That'll do,' he said and slapped the back of the shovel on the earth to mark his finish. I looked at my watch. It had barely gone three.

'Let's be going then,' said Eamon, lifting his knapsack onto one shoulder and throwing the shovel onto the other.

I hesitated. 'Shouldn't we say a prayer or something?' I asked. For a moment I thought Eamon was going to tell me to wise the fuck up, but he didn't. Instead he swung the spade off his shoulder again and planted the point in the soil, holding the shaft as if the hilt of a sword.

'You're right, Mick,' he said. '"Eternal rest grant unto him, O Lord, and let perpetual light shine upon him. May his soul, and the souls of all the faithful departed," particularly this night we remember Liam Finnegan and Peter McLaughlin, "rest in peace. Amen."'

We blessed ourselves and Eamon swung the spade back onto his shoulder. We hiked back up to the cars. Francie was waiting, with his shotgun broken over his forearm, smoking a cigarette. He offered us some. As we lit them he asked, 'It's done so?'

'Aye,' said Eamon, 'it's done.'

EPILOGUE

IT TRANSPIRED THAT after the disappearance of O'Riordain, presumed kidnapped and murdered by Crown forces, Francie Quinn was the most senior Republican figure in the parish, given his roles as acting head of the parish court and adjutant of the battalion.

Francie moved quickly to resolve the issue of the battalion running around town 'like a headless fucking chicken', by calling a meeting on Sunday afternoon and installing Eamon as officer commanding. It was meant to be an election, but most of the battalion was scared shiteless of Francie so when he proposed Eamon, no one objected.

I didn't see Eamon for a few days. He had decided to address some of the issues he had with O'Riordain by embarking his new command on a crash course of drill and field craft. On Tuesday morning, when it came time to bury Peter, Eamon made sure that the battalion provided a guard of honour. As they stood to rigid attention in the aisle of the church, Eamon and Francie made plain that they were rejecting O'Riordain and all his works.

I kept up attending Peter's office. Why, I am not sure. But I couldn't think of anything better to do. Francie was unavailable on the couple of occasions I tried to see him, but his wife did tell me, the last time I called at the house, that Father Crosby had agreed to join the parish court to replace Peter, so I should expect to hear from them in due course.

Bronagh seemed to have the same idea as myself and kept coming into the office. When I asked her what she was doing she told me she was trying to get Peter's papers in order so that the outstanding cases could be taken over by new legal representation. But for long periods as I sat alone in the kitchen I could hear her crying upstairs.

I had fuck all else to do so I returned to reading Holmes and Watson. In spite of my mind wandering to memories of a terrified man pissing himself all over me I managed to finish both the books I had borrowed by Wednesday evening. I decided to take this as an opportunity to see Sophia again.

Laoise was at her reception desk in the surgery as usual. Dr Hennessy was in with a patient. 'She shouldn't be too long. Do you want to wait?'

'Aye,' I said and I took a seat across from a mother and child already waiting to see the doctor.

'Hello again,' the mother said.

It took me a moment. 'Ah, Mrs Cassidy,' I said. She was looking exhausted with dark rings under her eyes. 'Stephen still poorly?'

Stephen had his face buried in his mother's shoulder, but he took a peek out at the mention of his name.

'He is,' she said.

'Still the cold, is it?'

'Ach, it's been one thing after another since he got that soaking last Tuesday. Cold, stomach bugs, coughs. Doctor said to come and see her again if he did not get better.'

'Tuesday?' I asked.

'What?'

'You said he got soaked out playing on Tuesday.'

'I know, when the master was off at Liam's wake, his own school friend.'

'I thought you said it was Monday he got his soaking, when the master came in late to school?'

'Well, whatever day it was, a big boy like Stephen should have had more sense than to be out playing in the rain, getting soaked to the skin.'

'But which day was it?'

'Oh God, I really don't remember any more. I don't suppose you know what it's like to try to keep five children fed and watered, do you? Sometimes I lose track of what day of the week it is.'

I felt my stomach heave and I broke into a cold sweat. 'Excuse me,' I said to Mrs Cassidy and lurched to my feet. I needed to get outside. I slammed the books down on Laoise's desk without another word and I made for the door. I barely managed to get outside before vomiting into the gutter.

I straightened myself and stumbled back until I found the support of the surgery wall, gulping cold air and trying to slow my racing heart. 'Tuesday,' I thought. Then I vomited again.

. . .

On Thursday afternoon Eamon came to call. Unusually, he appeared not to have shaved for a couple of days, but he seemed in good spirits.

'Cup of tea, Eamon?' I asked.

'Aye,' said Eamon. 'And set up the chess board.'

I did and made a king's pawn opening.

'How's it going?' he asked and echoed my king's pawn opening.

'I won't lie to you, Eamon, I've been better.'

'Still thinking about Sunday morning?'

'It's a hard thing to forget. Been having nightmares too.'

'Those will fade with time, I promise,' said Eamon. 'But they will never go away completely.'

'So how do I live with that?' I asked.

'Like the rest of us, I suppose,' said Eamon. 'At least you have the comfort of knowing what we did was necessary.'

'Was it, though?'

'What do you mean?'

'Remember your neighbour Mrs Cassidy who told us, Saturday morning, that her son had got ill playing in the rain last Monday morning, because Jack wasn't there.'

'I do.'

'I saw her again yesterday, in the doctor's surgery.'

'Young fella still not well?'

'No, but that's not my point.'

'What is?'

'She told me that it was Tuesday, not Monday, that Jack didn't show up for school, and that her young fella got soaked playing in the rain.'

Eamon sat back in his chair and looked at me. 'She told us Monday.'

'Now she's saying she doesn't remember which day of the week it was.'

Eamon was silent for what seemed like a long while. 'Maybe she was right the first time.'

'Maybe she wasn't.'

'That wasn't the only thing that led us to suspect Jack.'

'Maybe Crosby was, as you originally thought, spinning us a yarn to distract our attention from himself?'

'You think Sophia would not see through that sorta shite?'

'We believe what we want to believe. It's why we buy the snake-oil.'

'But why would Crosby help us the way he did then?'

'Fucked if I know. Maybe he is the one who gets off on killing. Maybe he got a thrill out of manipulating us into doing his bidding.'

'Jack did kill Peter.'

'What if Peter was an informer?'

'Peter was no fucking informer. That's something I'd bet my life on.'

'Well, it's something we bet Jack's life on, anyway.'

'And he did murder those peelers.'

'To inoculate his men from the revulsion of killing. The very thing you said to me when you told me I was the one had to kill Jack.'

'This is war, Mick. And war is a squalid and nasty business. You're an educated man. You know what Cicero said about war and the law.'

"'In times of war the laws fall silent.'"

'Exactly.'

'It's a bit convenient, though, isn't it?'

'What do you mean?'

'I mean, Jack seemed to take that observation as a carte blanche, to do whatever he pleased. Are we any better than him?'

'You know, I don't think Jack would ever have even asked that question.'

'But there was one thing he said was true: we really didn't give him a chance to answer the accusations against him.'

'Circumstances did sort of militate against that.'

'So it's not like the evidence against him was forensically tested. Maybe what he was saying was the truth, and we executed the wrong man for a murder he did not commit? That would make us no better than him. Maybe even worse.'

'There's a lot of "maybes" there.'

'You still think we did the right thing?'

'I don't believe we had any other choice. And I have seen fuckers like Jack in the war – people getting addicted to cruelty, just getting worse until they walk into a bullet.'

'An Irish bullet?'

'If that is what it takes.' Eamon took a mouthful of tea and looked at me. After a while he leaned back into the board and moved a bishop. 'When it is over,' he said, 'I will be against the death penalty again, and I promise you I will happily dedicate my life to establishing the sort of country that Peter dreamed of, with cleared slums and rule of law to our hearts' content. But sometimes in life, particularly in war, you do not have the choice between good and evil neatly presented to you. Instead, it's like that Agamemnon story you told me, you get a choice between two evils and the trick is to discern the lesser of them. Those that have never faced that dilemma never understand just how difficult that is, let alone what it's like to have to live with it afterwards.'

'I do not recall us doing that much agonising over it.'

'I saw you on Sunday morning, Mick. I see you now. And I do think that makes a difference. Sometimes it may be necessary to kill. It's them that don't doubt the morality of it, who don't question the necessity of it, it's them who are the dangerous ones. Like the crusaders and the Ironsides of history: morons with such certitude that murder comes naturally to them. But understand as well: we had an easy one this time, between risking the lives of more children in this parish, maybe in this county, and plugging a fucker who was a war criminal to start with.'

'If we killed the right man.'

'I believe we did.'

'Not even a grey-haired mammy to weep over him.'

'Aye. Now that the crisis has passed, Crosby has reverted to the strict observance of canon law, so there is no help from him here, but I do suspect that O'Riordain may have been responsible for his ma's untimely demise too.' Eamon moved another pawn.

'Why would you think that?'

'Just been reflecting on it these past days. If what Crosby said was true, that he had been abused by his father when he was growing up, it must have led to a considerable resentment against his ma, not protecting him and all.'

I am not sure if Eamon was saying this to make me feel a bit better, to emphasise that it was not an ordinary person that I had killed but a human monster… if what Crosby said was true.

But it didn't help much. Each time I closed my eyes I still saw O'Riordain's mutilated head in the light of a flashlight. And I knew that I had crossed that threshold willingly and on my own. Sometime during the previous week something that Casement had written had come to my mind. It was a protest against another colonial atrocity somewhere in Africa that I read in a newspaper around the time they hanged him. He'd written, '…we all on earth have a commission and a right to defend the weak against the strong, and to protest against brutality in any shape or form.' As I reflected on it in the middle of the nights when I could not sleep I had decided that no more children were going to get hurt if I could do anything about it. All I could do now was hope that I had indeed killed the right man.

'So, we're still good people. Is that what you are saying, Eamon? In spite of the grotesque thing we've done?'

'I suppose I'm saying, we're as good as can be expected, given the circumstances.'

We played on for a while in silence, staying just about level with each other on pieces taken.

'O'Riordain may be gone now, but he was not alone when he killed Peter,' I said. 'That fucker Shamey O'Neill was involved too, I'm certain of it.' I moved a knight.

'Aye. And maybe one or two others too. But worry not about Shamey the Hittite. This war is a long way from over and terrible things can happen in battle.'

It took me a moment to understand the allusion: Uriah the Hittite was the husband of King David's beloved mistress Bathsheba. When he became too much of an inconvenience King David sent Uriah to his commanding officer carrying sealed orders from the king that Uriah be placed in the most perilous part of the front lines and abandoned in the fighting so that he would be struck down.

I was surprised at the cold pleasure that the prospect gave me.

'So what's for me now?' I asked. 'Report to Francie?'

'No. I've spoken to Francie about this. We need to send some men for duty in the Flying Column. So I am going to assign you. I think it would be a good idea for you to make yourself scarce in these parts for a while.' Eamon, as was his wont, was continuing with an attack on my right flank.

'When do I leave?' I asked.

'At the weekend. Report to headquarters in Ballina. Francie will drive you and the others over.'

'Will they even take me, though? I've never fired a rifle in my life and I suspect my field craft is the worst in the battalion.'

'You're not the worst, Mick, and I think I can get you started on the operation and maintenance of a Lee-Enfield rifle before you go. And there will be plenty more training for you in the Flying Column. Kilroy, the commandant, is a humourless sort of fucker, but I appreciate his aggressive instincts.'

I didn't say anything but I moved my second knight, closing the trap on his king. 'Checkmate,' I said.

That caught Eamon unawares. 'Fucker!' he said, startled, and he looked at the board. Then he laughed and said, 'You cheeky little bastard,' and laughed again, a smile of admiration on his face. 'Well done,' he said and extended his hand to me. We shook over the board and he stood up.

'Going to miss you, Mick. But I'll see you before you go. Call round to ours tonight about seven. Me ma wants to make you dinner.'

He finished his tea and left the kitchen. I heard him clump down the hallway in his hobnailed boots and then the office door opened and he walked out onto the street.

As the door closed behind him I looked back at the checkmate. In the midst of everything, it was still one of the loveliest things I had ever seen.

Afterword

Anyone travelling through the county of Mayo in the province of Connaught looking for a town called Ballykennedy will be disappointed. It is located in a wholly imaginary part of the county between Ballina and Castlebar, a beautiful part of the world even with the absence of Ballykennedy, and the people of Mayo are as fine and hospitable as any you will ever have the good fortune to meet.

During the War of Independence there were four battalions of the IRA in County Mayo. Hence Jack O'Riordain commands the 5th (Ballykennedy) Battalion in the story. Though atrocities were committed on both sides in the struggle for Irish independence, those discussed in this story are wholly fictional. Anyone interested in further understanding of the course of the Irish Independence struggle could do much worse than Charles Townshend's two very fine books on the subject, *Easter 1916* and *The Republic*, Maurice Walsh's remarkable work, *Bitter Freedom – Ireland in a Revolutionary World 1918–23*, or Tim Pat Coogan's exemplary biography of Michael Collins.

Cahir Davitt, a young barrister and future president of the High Court, was appointed as a judge for the Republican courts in 1920, dealing with the Munster Circuit in the south. His account of his experiences in this role to the Irish Bureau of Military History is highly illuminating on this often over-looked aspect of the struggle.

I could find no record of Republican courts ever dealing with a case of murder. However, Davitt's counterpart for Connaught, Diarmuid Crowley, did undertake his first circuit in November 1920. This was ended abruptly at the sitting in Ballina, which was raided by Crown forces. Crowley was arrested and later sentenced to hard labour by a British court.

So, even if Peter, Eamon and Mick had managed to bring their case to trial at that circuit, it is highly unlikely justice would ever have been served.

Acknowledgements

First and most importantly, this book would never have seen the light of day had it not been for the faith and support of everyone who contributed to its publication. There are not enough words in the English language to say thanks properly.

I would never have even considered publishing this story were it not for the encouragement of the small cadre of readers who took it upon themselves to read earlier drafts of this book and give me comments upon it. So very special thanks to Meena Varma, Marty Sandler, Jill Heine, Martin Hubbard, Fergus Power, Sophia Tickell, David Hazafy, Joost Lina, Sophie Kramer, Kevin McCaul, Niamh Doran, Siobhan McQuade, Laoise NiBhrian, Vicky Brotherton, Eric 'the Code' Hanby, Nadine Finch, and Nick Kinsella.

I would also like to thank my long-suffering doctoral supervisors, Phyl Hughes and Gerry Johnson, under whose brutal tutelage I developed many of the ideas on ethics and morality that underpin this story. I hope this partially makes up to them for the dearth of academic papers from me over the years.

Philip Connor has been a brilliant and encouraging editor, and his advice and questions have been consistently wise and constructive and helped make *The Undiscovered Country* the best it could be. Alex Eccles has been a wise and enormously patient guide through the publication process. Justine Taylor's expert eye and comments have enriched every page. I am deeply grateful to all three. The remaining flaws, of course, are all my own.

Finally, as with so many things, this book would never have been completed without my beloved wife, Klara Skrivankova, whose constant support, encouragement and occasional intimidation spurred my efforts, cheered my doubts and calmed my soul through the long process from initial idea to final publication. It is to her this book is dedicated, with all my love.

Unbound is the world's first crowdfunding publisher, established in 2011.

We believe that wonderful things can happen when you clear a path for people who share a passion. That's why we've built a platform that brings together readers and authors to crowdfund books they believe in – and give fresh ideas that don't fit the traditional mould the chance they deserve.

This book is in your hands because readers made it possible. Everyone who pledged their support is listed below. Join them by visiting unbound.com and supporting a book today.

Jean Allain
Ann Allan
Mark Allison
Edie Anderson
Angola 1996–2001
Ursula Antwi-Boasiako
Barry Armstrong
Sinem Ayman
David Baillie
Kevin Bales
Jason Ballinger
Jo Becker
Jeroen Beirnaert
Ronnie Bendall
Cindy Berman
Sian Bevan

Urmila Bhoola
Andrew Bidnell
Marion Birch
Heather Blackwell
Caroline Blair
Sid Boggle
Andrew Bovarnick
Pam Bowen
Fintan Boyle
Julie Bozza
Ewen Bradley
Bernard Brannigan
Martin Brodetsky
Richard Brophy
Vicky Brotherton
Maggie Brown

Niall Browne
David Bryan
Suzanne Bunniss
David Burke
Olly Buston
John Buttery
Rebecca Buxton
Mark Campbell
Paraic Casey
Fergal Cassidy
Dara Castello
Erica Catlin
Parosha Chandran
Belinda Chiaramonte
Nathalie Clarke
Conor Clenaghan
Eithne Clenaghan
Finbar Clenaghan
Margaret Clenaghan
Mairead Clenaghan
   McGrane
James Cockayne
Mike Coffey
Laura Collier
Jacob Comenetz
Philip Connor
Nicola Conway
Laurence Cook
Caitlin Coslett

Sean Coughlan
Victoria Cox
Gary Craig
Niall Cranney
John Cropper
Jill Crowther
Estelle Currie
Donall Curtin
Mary Daly
Raj Dasani
Johanneke De Hoogh
Karin de Jonge
Tim Delaneuy
Christine Diaz
Justin Dillon
Harriet Dodd
Brian Doran
Eimear Doran
Geraldine Doran
Niamh Doran
Anne Douglas
Robert K. Drinan
Peter Duffy
Graham Duncan
Kevin Dwyer
Robert Eardley
Oliver Elgie
Gillian Fairfield
Paul Farrell

Amanda Ferguson

Nadine Finch

Sander Flight

Don Flynn

Christine Fosdal

Penny Fowler

Janet Fox

Stephen Gibson

Suzy Gillett

Samuel Godfrey

Dermot Goss

Joanne Greenway

Nicholas Grono

Margreet Groot

Kate Halff

Heather Hamill

Lois Hamilton

Kate Hammer

Nicholas Hammersley

Laura Hammond

Eric Hanby

Claire Hanna

Adrian Harris

Julia Hawkins

David Hazafy

Jill Heine

Oliver and Charlotte
   Herbert

Stephen Higgs

Peter Hobbins

Houtan Homayounpour

Eva Horelova

Kate Horner

Marketa Hronkova

Martin Hubbard

David Humphrey

Estelle Jacobs

Laura Jacobsen

Duncan Jepson

Denise Johnston

Leslie Johnston

Joyce Joles

Denis Jones

Aarti Kapoor

Riel Karmy-Jones

Mark Kelly

Tom Kelly

Rory Kenny

Dan Kieran

Manuel Kiewisch

James Kingston

Nick Kinsella

Andrew Kirkwood

Amelia Knott

Sue Knutton

Helene Kreysa

Katerina Ksvickova

Ray Lakeman

Bobby Lambert

Mavis Le Page Leathley

Sheri Lecker

Eric Lee

Joost Lina

Daisy Line

Sarah Lockyer

Agnieszka Lonska

Mary Lynch

Ruairí Mac Leanacháin

April Mackey Iliff

Marie Magill

Patrick Maguire

Virginie Mahin

Sean Mallon

Michael Mapstone

Mark Mathers

Tim May

Bartolome Mayol

Dermot Mc Cann

Eilish Mc Quade

Fiona Mc Quade

Tom Mcaleavey

Gavan McAlinden

Peter McAllister

Mary McAnulty

Kevin McCaul

Cormac McConnell

Calodagh McCumiskey

Garry McElherron

Debbie McGrath

Orla McGrory

Sue Yin McMahon

Anne McMurray

John McNally

Gerard McQuade

Joseph G McQuade

Siobhan McQuade

Eimear McQuade-Douglas

Jane Middlemiss

John Mitchinson

Mike Moran

Alison Morgan

John Morrison

Deirdre Mortell

Linda Murgatroyd

Aidan Murphy

Colin Murphy

Joanne Murphy & Conall
    McDevitt

Carlo Navato

Laoise Ni Bhriain

Mil Niepold

Grainne O' Toole

Chris O'Brien

Pat O'Brien

Peter O'Callaghan

Karen O'Connor

Paula O'Hare
Mark O'Neill
Jamie O'Nians
Sam O'Nians
Nuala O'Rourke
Rick O'Shea
John-Michael O'Sullivan
Ros O'Sullivan
Vinnie O'Dowd
Kevin O'Neill
Georgia Odd
Marek Okty
G Oommen
Philip Orr
Eric Ouellette
James Oury
Marcus Oxley
Nino Paichadze
Jane Pango
Geoff Patterson
Carrie Pemberton Ford
Mike Penrose
Rebecca Perlman
Virginija Petrauskaite
Cathy Pieters
Justin Pollard
Fergus Power
Dave Pratt
Programmeaneeanbook®

Trudi Purnell
Hugh Quarshie
Kevin Quinlan
Joel Quirk
Joanne Raisin
Alex Rawlings
Adil Rehman
Quentin Reynolds
Tara Reynor O'Grady
Kate Roberts
Thomas Rodgers
Fergus Rushe
Stephen Russell
Ben Rutledge
Timothy Ryan
Melonie Salam
Martin W Sandler
Natalie Sedacca
Chloe Setter
Ryna Sherazi
Cormac Sheridan
Ina Sjerps
Benjamin Skinner
Josef Skrivanek
Julie Skrivankova
Klara Skrivankova
Blanka and Josef
    Skrivankovi
Paul Sloan

Toni Smerdon
Emma Snow
Michael Solomon
Eamon Somers
Jodi Sonderman
Liliana Sorrentino
Eddie Spencer
James Spender
Howard Standen
Penny Street
Nina Stutler
Christine Svarer
Anna Swaithes
Sophia Tickell
Morgan Toner
Richard Trama
Steve Trent
Julia Trocme-Latter
Colin Udall
Krishna Upadhyaya

Marieke van Doorninck
Meena Varma
Vijay Varman
Louise Waite
Tim Waites
John Wallace
Julie Warren
Loretta Watson
Andy Way
Katy Webley
Paul Whitehouse
Luke Wilde
Rachel Wilshaw
Michelle Winthrop
Gretchen Woelfle
Emmett Woods
Paula Woods
Nicola Wright
Simon Wright
Jacqueline Zimowski